5066

GRAND SLAM:

13 Great Short Stories about Bridge

GRAND SLAM:

13 Great Short Stories about Bridge

Edited by

E. R. COLE and JAMES EDWARDS

G. P. Putnam's Sons, New York

To Mary Louise and Fronie

SBN: 399-11520-X

Library of Congress Catalog Number: 75-7673

PRINTED IN THE UNITED STATES OF AMERICA

Acknowledgments

E. R. Cole, James Edwards and G. P. Putnam's Sons wish to thank the following authors and publishers for permission to include copyrighted material:

"Sometimes It Relaxes You" by Sally Benson, copyright 1940 by F-R Publishing Corporation, reprinted from *Women and Children First* by Sally Benson, by permission of Random House, Inc., first published in *The New Yorker*.

"Bridge at Blades" by Ian Fleming, copyright 1955 by Glidrose Productions Ltd., reprinted from *Moonraker* by Ian Fleming, by permission of Macmillan Publishing Co., Inc., Glidrose Productions, Ltd., and Jonathan Cape Ltd.

"Jackie Plays 'The System' " by Alphonse Moyse, Jr., copyright 1954 by The Bridge World Magazine, Inc., reprinted by permission of Mrs. Alphonse Moyse.

"The Man Who Played Too Well" by Don Von Elsner, copyright 1968 by Behn-Miller Publishers, Inc., reprinted by permission of the author, first published in *Popular Bridge*.

"The Three Fat Women of Antibes" by W. Somerset Maugham, copyright 1933 by W. Somerset Maugham, reprinted from *Complete Short Stories* by W. Somerset Maugham, by permission of Doubleday and Company, Inc., the Estate of W. Somerset Maugham and William Heinemann, Ltd.

"Contract" by Ring Lardner, copyright 1929 by Harper's Bazaar, Inc., renewal copyright 1957 by Ellis A. Lardner, reprinted from *Round-Up* by Ring Lardner by permission of Charles Scribner's Sons.

"Last Board" by Ron Klinger, copyright 1971 by The Bridge World Magazine, Inc., reprinted by permission of the author.

"Character" by Stephen White, copyright 1940 by The Bridge World Magazine, Inc., reprinted by permission of the author.

"My Lady Love, My Dove" by Roald Dahl, copyright 1952 by Roald Dahl, reprinted from *Someone Like You* by Roald Dahl by permission of Alfred A. Knopf, Inc.

"The Great Kibitzers' Strike of 1926" by George S. Kaufman, copyright 1949 by *The New Yorker* Magazine, Inc., reprinted by permission.

"The Adventure of the Panamanian Girls" by Frank Thomas, copyright 1973 by Frank Thomas, reprinted from *Sherlock Holmes, Bridge Detective* by Frank Thomas and George Gooden, by permission of the author.

"The Exploits of Androcles MacThick: Or A Club to A-void" by Ernst T. Theimer, copyright 1964 by Modern Bridge, Inc., reprinted by permission of the author.

Contents

Foreword

One of the questions recently put to a hopeful—though perhaps overly confident—young TV contestant was "What is America's most popular card game?" The final word of the question had hardly been uttered when the reply came sailing back. It smacked of that fierce conviction one associates with a dogmatic proclamation: "Pinochle, of course!" The MC shook his head. "Rummy," the contestant ventured again, knowing it was now too late. "Poker?"

The MC smiled smugly. "Bridge, I'm afraid."

Had our young contestant considered for a moment the staggering number of books currently available on the subject of bridge as compared with those dealing with all other card games collectively, he would have had an easy victory. His imagination would have conjured up a sizable library in which hundreds of volumes promise the reader everything from a grasp of fundamentals in five easy lessons, to better bidding, better playing, better scores.

What he would not have found in that library is a volume of bridge stories, such as the one we are presenting here. It is—surprisingly, we think—entirely without precedent. And if that fact alone is not sufficient justification for the venture, the volume can speak for itself.

Thirteen stories are included (one for each card in a freshly dealt bridge hand) and thirteen authors. Our own Ring Lardner, George S. Kaufman, Sally Benson. England's Roald Dahl, Somerset Maugham, Ian Fleming. Australia's Ron Klinger. To name a few. The stories have previously appeared in magazines, in collections of individual authors, in anthologies. We found them occasionally outrageous, frequently exciting, always entertaining. But their quality and readability, while obvious requirements for inclusion, are by no means the reason they were assembled for the first time under one cover; that must be attributed rather to their common subject, which is the world of bridge, and the people who play it. The most bewildered tyro and the coolest Life Master will find enjoyment among these pages. So will the ninety-eight percent in between.

At least partially responsible for that enjoyment will be the reader's immediate recognition of many of the bridge-playing characters as his own partners and opponents. Who has not spent an evening with Frank (Frances) Hickson, the masterful theorist who could quote all the authorities ("The Three Fat Women of Antibes")? When Mrs. Pardee exclaims "Oh, Mr. Shevlin, why *didn't* you lead me a club? You *must* watch the discards! ("Contract")," we know we have been there before. And what about that goddess of the bridge table, Lucy Martin ("Character"), whose "handling of dummy reversal hands was a delight to behold," and whose "opening leads had become things of beauty"? Haven't we all—just once or twice—had the blissful experience of watching her in action.

If the characters in these stories differ widely from one another, so do the tones of the stories. Readers' tastes and moods are clearly not all alike, and those differences ought to be reflected in any anthology. We have tried our best to ensure this. There is, for example, the slick sophistication of "Bridge at Blades," considered by many to be the best card story ever written; the tortured idealism of "Last Board"; the familiar irony of "Sometimes It Relaxes You"; the tongue-in-cheekism of "The Great Kibitzers' Strike of 1926." There are even tales of master-detection, which bring Sherlock Holmes and Jake Winkman sleuthing in the bridge world ("The Adventure of the Panamanian Girls" and "The Man Who Played Too Well"). We wanted as much diversity of atmosphere in the collection as of characters.

The bridge hands in many of the stories are in layout form; in others, they have been integrated into the narrative. It won't take the reader long to note that their number and complexity vary a good deal from story to story—a fact which will certainly prove an additional prod.

One final point—well attested to in these pages—is that, for some players at any rate, bridge is very much a gambling game ("Good Guessing at Bridge," etc.). And, if there is any doubt about pulse rates (your own as well as the characters') rising with the stakes, try on, say, the Bond story for size.

As we see it, each of these thirteen stories is a winning trick. That should guarantee all of you a grand slam. So—on with the game! What do you open?

E.R.C.
J.E.

Sometimes It Relaxes You

By Sally Benson

RITA CROSBY looked anxiously at her husband. He stood in front of the bureau in his shirtsleeves, knotting his tie. His head was thrown back slightly and he was frowning. "Maybe we'd better not go," she said. "Where do you feel badly, *exactly?*"

"Nonsense!" Don Crosby said. He turned his head toward her and winced. "There's nothing the matter with me. Nothing really the matter. Of course, I don't feel like fighting a cage full of tigers, but I don't mind playing a little bridge with Ellen and George for a while."

"Is it your head?" she asked.

He felt his head carefully. "No," he told her, "it doesn't seem to be my head. It's more in back of my eyes, sort of."

"I don't think it could be your stomach, either," she said. "I mean, you enjoyed your dinner, didn't you?"

"I just thought I'd better eat. I wasn't really hungry." He took his coat from the back of the chair and slipped his arms into the sleeves. "Catches me in the back when I move," he said.

She went over to him and smoothed his collar. "Now, you're sure you think it's all right to go?"

"Do me good. Sometimes it relaxes you to go out."

She opened the top drawer of the bureau and took out a wool scarf. "Let me tuck this across your chest." She wrapped it snugly around his neck, smoothing it under his coat.

It was only two blocks from their apartment to the Elliots'. Mrs. Crosby took her husband's arm as they walked. From time to time she looked up at him and smiled, and patted his coat sleeve reassuringly.

At the Elliots', the bridge table was already set up in the living room and Ellen was counting the cards. "Hello, you two" she said. "There's a joker in here and I can't find it."

"Hello," Mrs. Crosby said. "We almost didn't come. Don isn't feeling up to snuff."

"Nonsense!" Mr. Crosby said.

George Elliot walked over to the window, pulled down the shade, and felt the radiator. "Plenty of heat," he said. "You don't want to monkey around if you're coming down with flu."

"Maybe you don't feel like playing," Mrs. Elliot said.

Mr. Crosby pulled a large upholstered chair over to the bridge table and sat down. He leaned over and spread the cards across the table. "Let's cut."

"Well, you're being a sport about it, I must say," Mrs. Elliot told him. She drew the ace of hearts. "Looks like I get the deal."

"Sure you're not in a draft now, Don?" George Elliot asked.

"Don't bother about me," Mr. Crosby answered. "I'm O.K."

"Marian Ford's mother is in the hospital with pneumonia," Mrs. Elliot said. "It's this change of weather."

Mrs. Crosby looked at her and shook her head. "What do you bid, Ellen?"

After the first rubber, which the Crosbys lost, Mr. Crosby asked if he might change his seat. "There's a sort of draft on the back of my neck," he said. "Unless you think the cards are running your way of the room."

"Oh, goodness! We're not superstitious," Mrs. Elliot told him. "But if you begin to feel too badly, just say the word and we can stop."

"It's nothing," Mr. Crosby said. He put his head in his hands and rubbed his eyes. "My eyeballs feel like lumps of coal."

It was a few minutes before he was settled on the couch, where Mr. Elliot had sat, with a cushion tucked in the small of his back. He lit a cigarette, took one puff, and put it out. "Tastes funny," he said.

"You don't mind if we keep the winning cards?" Mr. Elliot asked. "Probably nothing in the idea anyway."

The Crosbys won the second rubber, and Mr. Crosby took the cushion away from his back and tossed it to the end of the sofa. At the end of the third rubber, which they won also, he was sitting upright on the edge of the couch.

"Well," Mrs. Elliot said brightly, "I guess I was wrong about the cards. They do seem to be running one way."

Mr. Crosby laughed. "Nothing to those superstitions! But I can move just as well as not." He turned his head from side to side and experimented with two deep breaths.

It was generally agreed that he had better not move from the sofa. During the fourth rubber the Crosbys made one grand slam not vulnerable, one little slam vulnerable, and set the Elliots four tricks on a five-club bid.

Adding up the score, Mr. Crosby looked flushed, but it was a healthy flush. "Well, how about it?" he asked. "Want to try another?"

Mrs. Elliot picked up the cards. "Now, you just can't play any more," she said. "You've been a good enough sport as it is." She put the cards in their box and stood up. "I made a few sandwiches, if anybody is hungry. Would you like a little pineapple juice, Don? Sometimes it feels nice and cool to your throat."

"Nope," he answered. "Not for me, thanks. What kind of sandwiches you got, Ellen?"

"Ham," she said. "With mustard."

"That sounds great," he said. "As a matter of fact, I wasn't very hungry for dinner." He finished adding up the score. "Plus thirty-two. Three-twenty apiece. Not so bad for a sick man."

Mr. Elliot took a five-dollar bill, a one-dollar bill, and some change from his pocket and laid them on the table. The bills were new and crisp. Mr. Crosby picked them up and folded them neatly in his wallet. He jingled the silver in his hand. "Fortunes of war," he said pleasantly. His face was pink, his eyes were clear, and his hand was steady as he lit a cigarette. He smiled amiably at them all.

"I could do with a ham sandwich and a cup of coffee," he said. "Feed a cold and starve a fever."

He jingled the silver in his hand again and put it in his trouser pocket. "Plus thirty-two," he repeated. "Not so bad for a sick man."

Mrs. Elliot turned and left the room. The kitchen door was a swinging one and made no noise when she slammed it.

Bridge at Blades

By Ian Fleming

M. PAUSED while the next course came. With it arrived the champagne in a silver ice-bucket, and the small wicker-basket containing M.'s half-bottle of claret.

The wine-steward waited until they had delivered a favourable judgment on the wines and then moved away. As he did so a page came up to their table.

"Commander Bond?" he said.

Bond took the envelope that was handed to him and slit it open. He took out a thin paper packet and carefully opened it under the level of the table. It contained a white powder. He took a silver fruit knife off the table and dipped the tip of the blade into the packet so that about half its contents were transferred to the knife. He reached for his glass of champagne and tipped the powder into it.

"Now what?" said M. with a trace of impatience.

There was no hint of apology in Bond's face. It wasn't M. who was going to have to do the work that evening. Bond knew what he was doing. Whenever he had a job of work to do he would take infinite pains beforehand and leave as little as possible to chance. Then if something went wrong it was the unforeseeable. For that he accepted no responsibility.

"Benzedrine," he said. "I rang up my secretary before dinner and asked her to wangle some out of the surgery at Headquarters. It's what I shall need if I'm going to keep my wits about me tonight. It's apt to make one a bit overconfident, but that'll be a help too." He stirred the champagne with a scrap of toast so that the white powder whirled among the bubbles. Then he drank the mixture down with one long swallow. "It doesn't taste," said Bond, "and the champagne is quite excellent."

M. smiled at him indulgently. "It's your funeral," he said. "Now we'd better get on with our dinner. How were the cutlets?"

"Superb," said Bond. "I could cut them with a fork. The best English cooking is the best in the world—particularly at this time of the year. By the way, what stakes will we be playing for this evening? I don't mind very much. We ought to end up the winners. But I'd like to know how much it will cost Drax."

"Drax likes to play for what he calls 'One and One,' " said M., helping himself from the strawberries that had just been put on the table. "Modest-sounding stake, if you don't know what it stands for. In fact it's one tenner a hundred and one hundred pounds on the rubber."

"Oh," said Bond, respectfully. "I see."

"But he's perfectly happy to play for Two and Two or even Three and Three. Mounts up at those figures. The average rubber of bridge at Blades is about ten points. That's £200 at One and One. And the bridge here makes for big rubbers. There are no conventions, so there's plenty of gambling and bluffing. Sometimes it's more like poker. They're a mixed lot of players. Some of them are the best in England, but others are terribly wild. Don't seem to mind how much they lose. General Bealey, just behind us," M. made a gesture with his head, "doesn't know the reds from the blacks. Nearly always a few hundred down at the end of the week. Doesn't seem to care. Bad heart. No dependents. Stacks of money from jute. But Duff Sutherland, the scruffy-looking chap next to the Chairman, is an absolute killer. Makes a regular ten thousand a year out of the club. Nice chap. Wonderful card manners. Used to play chess for England."

M. was interrupted by the arrival of his marrowbone. It was placed upright in a spotless lace napkin on the silver plate. An ornate silver marrow-scoop was laid beside it.

After the asparagus, Bond had little appetite for the thin slivers of pineapple. He tipped the last of the ice-cold champagne into his glass. He felt wonderful. The effects of the benzedrine and champagne had more than offset the splendour of the food. For the first time he took his mind away from the dinner and his conversation with M. and glanced round the room.

It was a sparkling scene. There were perhaps fifty men in the room, the majority in dinner jackets all at ease with themselves and their surroundings, all stimulated by the peerless food and drink, all animated by a common interest—the prospect of high gambling, the grand slam, the ace pot, the key-throw in a 64 game at backgammon. There might be cheats or possible cheats amongst them, men who beat their wives, men with perverse instincts, greedy men, cowardly men, lying men; but the elegance of the room invested each one with a kind of aristocracy.

At the far end, above the cold table, laden with lobsters, pies, joints, and delicacies in aspic, Romney's unfinished full-length portrait of Mrs. Fitzherbert gazed provocatively across at Fragonard's *Jeu de Cartes*, the broad conversation piece which half filled the opposite wall above the Adam fireplace. Along the lateral walls, in the centre of each gilt-edged panel, was one of the rare engravings of the Hell-Fire Club in which each figure is shown making a minute gesture of scatological or magical significance. Above, marrying the walls into the ceiling, ran a frieze in plaster relief of carved nuns and swags interrupted at intervals by the capitals of the fluted pilasters which framed the windows and the tall double doors, the latter delicately carved with a design showing the Tudor Rose interwoven with a ribbon effect.

The central chandelier, a cascade of crystal ropes terminating in a broad basket of strung quartz, sparkled warmly above the white damask tablecloths and George IV silver. Below, in the centre of each table, branched candlesticks distributed the golden light of three candles, each surmounted by a red silk shade, so that the faces of the diners shone with a convivial warmth which glossed over the occasional chill of an eye or cruel twist of a mouth.

Even as Bond drank in the warm elegance of the scene, some of the groups began to break up. There was a drift towards the door accompanied by an exchange of challenges, side-bets, and exhortations to hurry up and get down to business. Sir Hugo Drax, his hairy red face shining with cheerful anticipation, came towards them with Meyer in his wake.

"Well, gentlemen," he said jovially as he reached their table. "Are the lambs ready for the slaughter and the geese for the plucking?" He grinned and in wolfish pantomime drew a finger across his throat. "We'll go ahead and lay out the axe and the basket. Made your wills?"

"Be with you in a moment," said M. edgily. "You go along and stack the cards."

Drax laughed. "We shan't need any artificial aids," he said. "Don't be long." He turned and made for the door. Meyer enveloped them in an uncertain smile and followed him.

M. grunted. "We'll have coffee and brandy in the card room," he said to Bond. "Can't smoke here. Now then. Any final plans?"

"I'll have to fatten him up for the kill, so please don't worry if I seem to be betting high," said Bond. "We'll just have to play our normal game till the time comes. When it's his deal, we'll have to be careful. Of course, he can't alter the cards and there's no reason why he shouldn't deal us good hands, but he's bound to bring off some pretty remarkable coups. Do you mind if I sit on his left?"

"No," said M. "Anything else?"

Bond reflected for a moment. "Only one thing, sir," he said. "When the time comes, I shall take a white handkerchief out of my coat pocket. That will mean that you are about to be dealt a Yarborough. Would you please leave the bidding of the hand to me?"

Drax and Meyer were waiting for them. They were leaning back in their chairs, smoking Cabinet Havanas. On the small tables beside them there was coffee and large balloons of brandy. As M. and Bond came up, Drax was tearing the paper cover off a new pack of cards. The other pack was fanned out across the green baize in front of him.

"Ah, there you are," said Drax. He leant forward and cut a card. They all followed suit. Drax won the cut and elected to stay where he was and take the red cards.

Bond sat down on Drax's left.

M. beckoned to a passing waiter. "Coffee and the club

brandy," he said. He took out a thin black cheroot and offered one to Bond, who accepted it. Then he picked up the red cards and started to shuffle them.

"Stakes?" asked Drax, looking at M. "One and One? Or more? I'll be glad to accommodate you up to Five and Five."

"One and One'll be enough for me," said M. "James?"

Drax cut in. "I suppose your guest knows what he's in for?" he asked sharply.

Bond answered for M. "Yes," he said briefly. He smiled at Drax. "And I feel rather generous tonight. What would you like to take off me?"

"Every penny you've got," said Drax cheerfully. "How much can you afford?"

"I'll tell you when there's none left," said Bond. He suddenly decided to be ruthless. "I'm told that Five and Five is your limit. Let's play for that."

Almost before the words were out of his mouth he regretted them. £50 a hundred! £500 side bets! Four bad rubbers would be double his income for a year. If something went wrong he'd look pretty stupid. Have to borrow from M. and M. wasn't a particularly rich man. Suddenly he saw that this ridiculous game might end in a very nasty mess. He felt the prickle of sweat on his forehead. That damned benzedrine. And, for him of all people to allow himself to be needled by a blustering loudmouthed bastard like Drax. And he wasn't even on a job. The whole evening was a bit of social pantomime that meant less than nothing to him. Even M. had only been dragged into it by chance. And all of a sudden he'd let himself be swept up into a duel with this multimillionaire, into a gamble for literally all Bond possessed, for the simple reason that the man had got filthy manners and he'd wanted to teach him a lesson. And supposing the lesson didn't come off? Bond cursed himself for an impulse that earlier in the day would have seemed unthinkable. Champagne and benzedrine! Never again.

Drax was looking at him in sarcastic disbelief. He turned to M., who was still unconcernedly shuffling the cards. "I suppose your guest is good for his commitments," he said. Unforgivably.

Bond saw the blood rush up M.'s neck and into his face. M. paused for an instant in his shuffling. When he continued Bond noticed that his hands were quite calm. M. looked up and took the cheroot very deliberately out from between his teeth. His voice was perfectly controlled. "If you mean 'Am I good for my guest's commitments?'," he said coldly, "the answer is 'yes.' "

He cut the cards to Drax with his left hand, and with his right knocked the ash off his cheroot into the copper ashtray in the corner of the table. Bond heard the faint hiss as the burning ash hit the water.

Drax squinted sideways at M. He picked up the cards. "Of course, of course," he said hastily. "I didn't mean . . ." He left the sentence unfinished and turned to Bond. "Right, then," he said, looking rather curiously at Bond. "Five and Five it is. Meyer," he turned to his partner, "how much would you like to take? There's Six and Six to cut up."

"One and One's enough for me, Hugger," said Meyer apologetically. "Unless you'd like me to take some more." He look anxiously at his partner.

"Of course not," said Drax. "I like a high game. Never get enough on generally. Now then," he started to deal. "Off we go."

And suddenly Bond didn't care about the high stakes. Suddenly all he wanted to do was to give this hairy ape the lesson of his life, give him a shock which would make him remember this evening forever, remember Bond, remember M., remember the last time he would cheat at Blades, remember the time of day, the weather outside, what he had had for dinner.

For all its importance, Bond had forgotten the Moonraker. This was a private affair between two men.

As he watched the casual downward glance at the cigarette case between the two hands and felt the cool memory ticking up the card values as they passed over its surface, Bond cleared his mind of all regrets, absolved himself of all blame for what was about to happen, and focused his attention on the game. He settled himself more comfortably into his chair and rested his hands on the padded leather arms. Then he took the thin cheroot from between his teeth, laid it on the burnished copper surround of the ashtray beside him and reached for his coffee. It was very black and strong. He emptied the cup and picked up the balloon glass with its fat measure of pale brandy. As he sipped it and then drank again, more deeply, he looked over the rim at M. M. met his eye and smiled briefly.

"Hope you like it," he said. "Comes from one of the Rothschild estates at Cognac. About a hundred years ago one of the family bequeathed us a barrel of it every year in perpetuity. During the war they hid a barrel for us every year and then sent us over the whole lot in 1945. Ever since then we've been drinking doubles. And," he gathered up his cards, "now we shall have to concentrate."

Bond picked up his hand. It was average. A bare two-and-a-half quick tricks, the suits evenly distributed. He reached for his cheroot and gave it a final draw, then killed it in the ashtray.

"Three clubs," said Drax.

No bid from Bond.

Four clubs from Meyer.

No bid from M.

Hm, thought Bond. He's not quite got the cards for a game call this time. Shut-out calls—knows that his partner has got a bare raise. M. may have got a perfectly good bid. We may have all the hearts between us, for instance. But M. never gets a bid. Presumably they'll make four clubs.

They did, with the help of one finesse through Bond. M. turned out not to have had hearts, but a long string of diamonds, missing only the king, which was in Meyer's hand and would have been caught. Drax didn't have nearly enough length for a three call. Meyer had the rest of the clubs.

Anyway, thought Bond as he dealt the next hand, we were lucky to escape without a game call.

Their good luck continued. Bond opened a no trump, was put up to three by M., and they made it with an overtrick. On Meyer's deal they went one down in five diamonds, but on the next hand M. opened four spades and Bond's three small trumps and an outside king, queen were all M. needed for the contract.

First rubber to M. and Bond. Drax looked annoyed. He had lost £900 on the rubber, and the cards seemed to be running against them.

"Shall we go straight on?" he asked. "No point in cutting."

M. smiled across at Bond. The same thought was in both their minds. So Drax wanted to keep the deal. Bond shrugged his shoulders.

"No objections," said M. "These seats seem to be doing their best for us."

"Up to now," said Drax, looking more cheerful.

And with reason. On the next hand he and Meyer bid and made a small slam in spades that required two hair-raising finesses, both of which Drax, after a good deal of pantomime and hemming and hawing, negotiated smoothly, each time commenting loudly on his good fortune.

"Hugger, you're wonderful," said Meyer fulsomely. "How the devil do you do it?"

Bond thought it time to sow a tiny seed. "Memory," he said.

Drax looked at him, sharply. "What do you mean, memory?" he said. "What's that got to do with taking a finesse?"

"I was going to add, 'and card sense,'" said Bond smoothly. "They're the two qualities that make great card-players."

"Oh," said Drax slowly. "Yes, I see." He cut the cards to Bond, and as Bond dealt he felt the other man's eyes examining him carefully.

The game proceeded at an even pace. The cards refused to get hot, and no one seemed inclined to take chances. M. doubled Meyer in an incautious four-spade bid and got him two down vulnerable, but on the next hand Drax went out with a lay-down three no trumps. Bond's win on the first rubber was wiped out and a bit more besides.

"Anyone care for a drink?" asked M. as he cut the cards to Drax for the third rubber. "James. A little more champagne. The second bottle always tastes better."

"I'd like that very much," said Bond.

The waiter came. The others ordered whiskies and sodas.

Drax turned to Bond. "This game needs livening up," he said. "A hundred we win this hand." He had completed the deal, and the cards lay in neat piles in the centre of the table.

Bond looked at him. The damaged eye glared at him redly. The other was cold and hard and scornful. There were beads of sweat on either side of the large, beaky nose.

Bond wondered if he was having a fly thrown over him to see if he was suspicious of the deal. He decided to leave the man in doubt. It was a hundred down the drain, but it would give him an excuse for increasing the stakes later.

"On your deal?" he said with a smile. "Well . . ." He weighed imaginary chances. "Yes. All right." An idea seemed to come to him. "And the same on the next hand. If you like," he added.

"All right, all right," said Drax impatiently. "If you want to throw good money after bad."

"You seem very certain about this hand," said Bond indifferently, picking up his cards. They were a poor lot and he had no answer to Drax's opening no trump except to double it. The bluff had no effect on Drax's partner. Meyer said, "Two no trumps," and Bond was relieved when M., with no long suit, said, "No bid." Drax left it in two no trumps and made the contract.

"Thanks," he said with relish, and wrote carefully on his score. "Now let's see if you can get it back."

Much to his annoyance, Bond couldn't. The cards still ran for Meyer and Drax, and they made three hearts and the game.

Drax was pleased with himself. He took a long swallow at his whiskey and soda and wiped down his face with his bandanna handkerchief.

"God is with the big battalions," he said jovially. "Got to have the cards as well as play them. Coming back for more, or had enough?"

Bond's champagne had come and was standing beside

him in its silver bucket. There was a glass goblet three-quarters full beside it on the side table. Bond picked it up and drained it, as if to give himself Dutch courage. Then he filled it again.

"All right," he said thickly, "a hundred on the next two hands."

And promptly lost them both, and the rubber.

Bond suddenly realized that he was nearly £1,500 down. He drank another glass of champagne. "Save trouble if we just double the stakes on this rubber," he said rather wildly. "All right with you?"

Drax had dealt and was looking at his cards. His lips were wet with anticipation. He looked at Bond, who seemed to be having difficulty lighting his cigarette. "Taken," he said quickly. "A hundred pounds a hundred, and a thousand on the rubber." Then he felt he could risk a touch of sportsmanship. Bond could hardly cancel the bet now. "But I seem to have got some good tickets here," he added. "Are you still on?"

"Of course, of course," said Bond, clumsily picking up his hand. "I made the bet, didn't I?"

"All right then," said Drax with satisfaction. "Three no trumps here."

He made four.

Then, to Bond's relief, the cards turned. Bond bid and made a small slam in hearts, and on the next hand M. ran out in three no trumps.

Bond grinned cheerfully into the sweating face. Drax was picking angrily at his nails. "Big battalions," said Bond, rubbing it in.

Drax growled something and busied himself with the score.

Bond looked across at M., who was putting a match, with evident satisfaction at the way the game had gone, to his second cheroot of the evening, an almost unheard of indulgence.

" 'Fraid this'll have to be my last rubber," said Bond. "Got to get up early. Hope you'll forgive me."

M. looked at his watch. "It's past midnight," he said. "What about you, Meyer?"

Meyer, who had been a silent passenger for most of the evening, and who had the look of a man caught in a cage with a couple of tigers, seemed relieved at being offered a chance of making his escape. He leapt at the idea of getting back to his quiet flat in Albany and the soothing companionship of his collection of Battersea snuffboxes.

"Quite all right with me, Admiral," he said quickly. "What about you, Hugger? Nearly ready for bed?"

Drax ignored him. He looked up from his score-sheet at Bond. He noticed the signs of intoxication. The moist forehead, the black comma of hair that hung untidily over the right eyebrow, the sheen of alcohol in the grey-blue eyes.

"Pretty miserable balance so far," he said. "I make it you win a couple of hundred or so. Of course if you want to run out of the game you can. But how about some fireworks to finish up with? Treble the stakes on the last rubber? Fifteen and fifteen? Historic match. Am I on?"

Bond looked at him. He paused before answering. He wanted Drax to remember every detail of this last rubber, every word that had been spoken, every gesture.

"Well," said Drax impatiently. "What about it?"

Bond looked into the cold left eye in the flushed face. He spoke to it alone.

"One hundred and fifty pounds a hundred, and fifteen hundred pounds on the rubber," he said distinctly. "You're on."

There was a moment's silence at the table. It was broken by the agitated voice of Meyer.

"Here I say," he said anxiously. "Don't include me in on this, Hugger." He knew it was a private bet with Bond, but he wanted to show Drax that he was thoroughly nervous about the whole affair. He saw himself making some ghastly mistake that would cost his partner a lot of money.

"Don't be ridiculous, Max," said Drax harshly. "You play your hand. This is nothing to do with you. Just an enjoyable little bet with our rash friend here. Come along, come along. My deal, Admiral."

M. cut the cards and the game began.

Bond lit a cigarette with hands that had suddenly become quite steady. His mind was clear. He knew exactly what he had to do, and when, and he was glad that the moment of decision had come.

He sat back in his chair, and for a moment he had the impression that there was a crowd behind him at each elbow, and that faces were peering over his shoulder, waiting to see his cards. He somehow felt that the ghosts were friendly, that they approved of the rough justice that was about to be done.

He smiled as he caught himself sending this company of dead gamblers a message, that they should see that all went well.

The background noise of the famous gaming room broke in on his thoughts. He looked round. In the middle of the long room, under the central chandelier, there were several onlookers round the poker game. "Raise you a hundred." "And a hundred." "And a hundred." "Damn you. I'll look." And a shout of triumph followed by a hubbub of comment. In the distance he could hear the rattle of a croupier's rake against the counters at the Shemmy game. Nearer at hand, at his end of the room, there were three other tables of bridge over which the smoke of cigars and cigarettes rose towards the barralled ceiling.

Nearly every night for more than a hundred and fifty years there had been just such a scene, he reflected, in this famous room. The same cries of victory and defeat, the same dedicated faces, the same smell of tobacco and drama. For Bond, who loved gambling, it was the most exciting spectacle in the world. He gave it a last glance to fix it all in his mind, and then he turned back to his table.

He picked up his cards and his eyes glittered. For once, on Drax's deal, he had a cast-iron game hand; seven spades with the four top honours, the ace of hearts, and the ace, king of diamonds. He looked at Drax. Had he and Meyer got the clubs? Even so Bond could overbid. Would Drax try to force him too high and risk a double? Bond waited.

"No bid," said Drax, unable to keep the bitterness of his private knowledge of Bond's hand out of his voice.

"Four spades," said Bond.

No bid from Meyer; from M.; reluctantly from Drax.

M. provided some help, and they made five.

One hundred and fifty points below the line. A hundred above for honours.

"Humph," said a voice at Bond's elbow. He looked up. It was Basildon. His game had finished, and he had strolled over to see what was happening on this separate battlefield.

He picked up Bond's score-sheet and looked at it.

"That was a bit of a beetle-crusher," he said cheerfully. "Seems you're holding the champions. What are the stakes?"

Bond left the answer to Drax. He was glad of the diversion. It could not have been better timed. Drax had cut the blue cards to him. He married the two halves and put the pack just in front of him, near the edge of the table.

"Fifteen and fifteen. On my left," said Drax.

Bond heard Basildon draw in his breath.

"Chap seemed to want to gamble, so I accommodated him. Now he goes and gets all the cards . . ."

Drax grumbled on.

Across the table, M. saw a white handkerchief materialize in Bond's right hand. M.'s eyes narrowed. Bond seemed to wipe his face with it. M. saw him glance sharply at Drax and Meyer, then the handkerchief was back in his pocket.

A blue pack was in Bond's hands, and he had started to deal.

"That's a hell of a stake," said Basildon. "We once had a thousand-pound side-bet on a game of bridge. But that was in the rubber boom before the '14-18 war. Hope nobody's going to get hurt." He meant it. Very high stakes in a private game generally led to trouble. He walked round and stood between M. and Drax.

Bond completed the deal. With a touch of anxiety he picked up his cards.

He had nothing but five clubs to the ace, queen, ten, and eight small diamonds to the queen.

It was all right. The trap was set.

He almost felt Drax stiffen as the big man thumbed through his cards, and then, unbelieving, thumbed them through again. Bond knew that Drax had an incredibly good hand. Ten certain tricks, the ace, king of diamonds, the four top honours in spades, the four top honours in hearts, and the king, knave, nine of clubs.

Bond had dealt them to him—in the Secretary's room before dinner.

Bond waited, wondering how Drax would react to the huge hand. He took an almost cruel interest in watching the greedy fish come to the lure.

Drax exceeded his expectations.

Casually he folded his hand and laid it on the table. Nonchalantly he took the flat carton out of his pocket, selected a cigarette, and lit it. He didn't look at Bond. He glanced up at Basildon.

"Yes," he said, continuing the conversation about their stakes. "It's a high game, but not the highest I've ever played. Once played for two thousand a rubber in Cairo. At the Mahomet Ali, as a matter of fact. They've really got guts there. Often bet on every trick as well as on the game and rubber. Now," he picked up his hand and looked slyly at Bond. "I've got some good tickets here. I'll admit it. But then you may have too, for all I know." (Unlikely, you old shark, thought Bond, with three of the ace-kings in your own hand.) "Care to have something extra just on this hand?"

Bond made a show of studying his cards with the minuteness of someone who is nearly very drunk. "I've got a promising lot too," he said thickly. "If my partner fits and the cards lie right I might make a lot of tricks myself. What are you suggesting?"

"Sounds as if we're pretty evenly matched," lied Drax. "What do you say to a hundred a trick on the side? From what you say that shouldn't be too painful."

Bond looked thoughtful and rather fuddled. He took another careful look at his hand, running through the cards one by one. "All right," he said. "You're on. And frankly you've made me gamble. You've obviously got a big hand, so I must shut you out and chance it."

Bond looked blearily across at M. "Pay your losses on

this one, partner," he said. "Here we go. Er—seven clubs."

In the dead silence that followed, Basildon, who had seen Drax's hand, was so startled that he dropped his whiskey and soda on the floor. He looked dazedly down at the broken glass and let it lie.

Drax said, "What?" in a startled voice and hastily ran through his cards again for reassurance.

"Did you say grand slam in clubs?" he asked, looking curiously at his obviously drunken opponent. "Well, it's your funeral. What do you say, Max?"

"No bid," said Meyer, feeling in the air the electricity of just that crisis he had hoped to avoid. Why the hell hadn't he gone home before this last rubber? He groaned inwardly.

"No bid," said M., apparently unperturbed.

"Double." The word came viciously out of Drax's mouth. He put down his hand and looked cruelly, scornfully at this tipsy oaf who had at last, inexplicably, fallen into his hands.

"That mean you double the side bets too?" asked Bond.

"Yes," said Drax greedily. "Yes. That's what I meant."

"All right," said Bond. He paused. He looked at Drax and not at his hand. "Redouble. The contract and the side bets. £400 a trick on the side."

It was at that moment that the first hint of a dreadful, incredible doubt entered Drax's mind. But again he looked at his hand, and again he was reassured. At the very worst he couldn't fail to make two tricks.

A muttered "No bid" from Meyer. A rather strangled "No bid" from M. An impatient shake of the head from Drax.

Basildon stood, his face very pale, looking intently across the table at Bond.

Then he walked slowly round the table, scrutinizing all the hands. What he saw was this:

BOND
♢ Queen, 8, 7, 6, 5, 4, 3, 2
♣ Ace, queen, 10, 8, 4

DRAX
♠ Ace, king, queen, knave
♡ Ace, king, queen, knave
♢ Ace, king
♣ King, knave, 9

MEYER
♠ 6, 5, 4, 3, 2
♡ 10, 9, 8, 7, 2
♢ Knave, 10, 9

M.
♠ 10, 9, 8, 7
♡ 6, 5, 4, 3
♣ 7, 6, 5, 3, 2

And suddenly Basildon understood. It was a lay-down Grand Slam for Bond against any defence. Whatever Meyer led, Bond must get in with a trump in his own hand or on the table. Then, in between clearing trumps, finessing of course against Drax, he would play two rounds of diamonds, trumping them in dummy and catching Drax's ace and king in the process. After five plays he would be left with the remaining trumps and six winning diamonds. Drax's aces and kings would be totally valueless.

It was sheer murder.

Basildon, almost in a trance, continued round the table and stood between M. and Meyer so that he could watch Drax's face, and Bond's. His own face was impassive, but his hands, which he had stuffed into his trouser pockets so that they would not betray him, were sweating. He waited, almost fearfully, for the terrible punishment that Drax was about to receive—thirteen separate lashes whose scars no card-player would ever lose.

"Come along, come along," said Drax impatiently. "Lead something, Max. Can't be here all night."

You poor fool, thought Basildon. In ten minutes you'll wish that Meyer had died in his chair before he could pull out that first card.

In fact, Meyer looked as if at any moment he might have a stroke. He was deathly pale, and the perspiration was dropping off his chin on to his shirt front. For all he knew, his first card might be a disaster.

At last, reasoning that Bond might be void in his own long suits, spades and hearts, he led the knave of diamonds.

It made no difference what he led, but when M.'s hand went down showing chicane in diamonds, Drax snarled across at his partner. "Haven't you got anything else, you damn' fool? Want to hand it to him on a plate? Whose side are you on anyway?"

Meyer cringed into his clothes. "Best I could do, Hugger," he said miserably, wiping his face with his handkerchief.

But by this time Drax had got his own worries.

Bond trumped on the table, catching Drax's king of diamonds, and promptly led a club. Drax put up his nine. Bond took it with his ten and led a diamond, trumping it on the table. Drax's ace fell. Another club from the table, catching Drax's knave.

Then the ace of clubs.

As Drax surrendered his king, for the first time he saw what might be happening. His eyes squinted anxiously at Bond, waiting fearfully for the next card. Had Bond got the diamonds? Hadn't Meyer got them guarded? After all, he had opened with them. Drax waited, his cards slippery with sweat.

Morphy, the great chess player, had a terrible habit. He would never raise his eyes from the game until he knew his opponent could not escape defeat. Then he would slowly lift his great head and gaze curiously at the man across the board. His opponent would feel the gaze and would slowly, humbly raise his eyes to meet Morphy's. At that moment he would know that it was no good continuing the game. The eyes of Morphy said so. There was nothing left but surrender.

Now, like Morphy, Bond lifted his head and looked straight into Drax's eyes. Then he slowly drew out the queen of diamonds and placed it on the table. Without waiting for Meyer to play he followed it, deliberately, with the 8, 7, 6, 5, 4, and the two winning clubs.

Then he spoke. "That's all, Drax," he said quietly, and sat slowly back in his chair.

Drax's first reaction was to lurch forward and tear Meyer's cards out of his hand. He faced them on the table, scrabbling feverishly among them for a possible winner.

Then he flung them back across the baize.

His face was dead white, but his eyes blazed redly at Bond. Suddenly he raised one clenched fist and crashed it on the table among the pile of impotent aces and kings and queens in front of him.

Very low, he spat the words at Bond. "You're a ch—"

"That's enough, Drax." Basildon's voice came across the table like a whiplash. "None of that talk here. I've been watching the whole game. Settle up. If you've got any complaints, put them in writing to the Committee."

Drax got slowly to his feet. He stood away from his chair and ran a hand through his wet red hair. The colour came slowly back into his face, and with it an expression of cunning. He glanced down at Bond, and there was in his good eye a contemptuous triumph which Bond found curiously disturbing.

He turned to the table. "Good night, gentlemen," he said, looking at each of them with the same oddly scornful expression. "I owe about £15,000. I will accept Meyer's addition."

He leant forward and picked up his cigarette-case and lighter.

Then he looked again at Bond and spoke very quietly, the red moustache lifting slowly from the splayed upper teeth.

"I should spend the money quickly, Commander Bond," he said.

Then he turned away from the table and walked swiftly out of the room.

Jackie Plays "The System"

By Alphonse Moyse, Jr.

IT WASN'T a really *bad* dinner. True, the pot roast was scorched and the potatoes were a little hard, but that was all, so there was no actual proof that my wife Jackie was not in the best of humors. There was only that aura of suppressed expectancy to go by; any husband past the freshman year would have known she was waiting, just *waiting*, for me to complain. So of course I munched with gusto and kept quiet.

"Everything all right?" she cooed, with the merest glance toward the pot roast.

"Fine, really fine," I said, chewing manfully. "Why?"

"Nothing!" She drew a long, long breath, then placed her knife and fork in meticulous position on her plate.

"Why," she hissed from between gritted teeth, "wasn't I asked to play on the Cavendish team against the Regency Club?"

"Oh," I said. "So that's it."

"That's what?" Her eyes dared me to answer.

"I sensed that you were, er, upset," I said carefully, keeping my eyes away from the so-called food.

She h'mphed. "I have *never* been so insulted! Do you know what I'm going to do? I'm going to *resign!*"

"From what?" I asked innocently.

"From the Cavendish Club, of course!"

I was quite equable about it. All I said was: "Now, how can you do that, darling? You're not a member."

"That's ridiculous. I'm your wife, aren't I?"

"You are, definitely."

"And *you're* a member, aren't you?"

I admitted it.

"Well?" she demanded.

It was not so much this time-honored feminine summation, that always unanswerable "Well?" that engaged my mind—no, I was fascinated by the delicate problem suggested, and I resolved to ask Lee Hazen, the eminent barrister, for an opinion on this point. Could a wife, not herself a member of a club, resign the membership conferred on her by marriage? My thoughts leaped ahead—to Jackie presenting her resignation to the Board of Governors. "You can't resign," says the Board. "You're not a member." "Oh," Jackie says, "so you refuse to accept my resignation." "No, we don't refuse," says the Board. "Then you do accept it?" Jackie pursues relentlessly. "No, we don't accept it," says the Board, a great stickler for parliamentary regularity.

I was getting myself dizzy.

"I should *think*," said Jackie, "that you would *protect me* from such insults."

Reflecting that no great sacrifice would be involved, I laid down my own knife and fork. "Now really. I wasn't on the selection committee, you know. And though I'd fight lions and tigers for you—"

"You could have *insisted* on having me as your partner."

"Honestly, I couldn't. Why you know I like to play with you, and—"

"Okay-this-weekend-at-the-Atlantic-City-tournament." The words came out in exactly 3.2 seconds.

As we settled into the North-South seats at our first table in the mixed pairs, Jackie said casually, "Let's play sort of Roth-Stonish. Weak jump responses, weak overcalls, weak openings in third and fourth position—"

"Baby," I said, "the picture is clear. We'll do everything weak."

"Weak two-bids, weak minor-suit bids, weak—"

"That does it," I told her. "Now, as of this moment, I haven't the strength to hold 13 cards."

"Well, just *remember*, that's all. There must be *some* reason for all this talk about the Roth-Stone."

"My dear," I said, "I realize that Harper's Bazaar has better fashions, but if you could spare the time to read *The Bridge World* you would find many *different* reasons put out for—"

"Toby Stone told me privately that if I played the system I'd be a Life Master in no time."

"Well, some people—not me, of course—consider Stoney a shade biased, but—"

The arrival of our first opponents put an end to this dialogue, and we all reached for our hands.

South dealer
Both sides vulnerable

NORTH
♠ K Q J 10 8 7 5
♡ —
◇ 9 2
♣ A 9 8 5

WEST		EAST
♠ 6 3 2		♠ A 9 4
♡ J 10 9 5		♡ Q 8 6
◇ Q 10 8 7		◇ K J
♣ 6 4		♣ K Q J 10 7

SOUTH
♠ —
♡ A K 7 4 3 2
◇ A 6 5 4 3
♣ 3 2

I started off, innocent as a babe, with one heart on the South cards, and the auction rolled swiftly along:

SOUTH	WEST	NORTH	EAST
1 ♡	Pass	2 ♠	3 ♣
Pass	Pass	D'ble	PASS
Pass	Pass		

I opened the heart king, got the nine of diamonds from Jackie, and continued with the ace and seven of hearts. Jackie ruffed and led the spade king. I exterminated East's ace—trying to ignore my RHO's withering glare—and shifted to the ace and another diamond. My killer-wife ruffed, cashed the queen and jack of spades, and later produced the ace of trumps to make the penalty a good round 1400 points.

Two unrelated things then occurred simultaneously: the very blond lady who sat East reached over and studied our score-card which purported to announce our system; and Jackie asked anxiously, "We couldn't have made a slam, could we?"

I murmured, "I don't think so, dear, though I always hesitate to say what *you* might do at any contract," just as East completed her survey and fixed a glittering eye on Jackie. That is, I was under the distinct impression that one glittering eye was fixed on Jackie and one on me. "May I ask," she said, spacing her words metronomically, "what this notation on your score-card means? 'Modified Roth-Stone,' it says, and I seem to read, among other things, '*weak* jump responses.' " (The italics were hers.) "I wouldn't call the North hand exactly weak!"

"Oh, you wouldn't," said Jackie. "Well, I would. A bad misfit with my partner's hand—with *both* of his suits—only one ace, and no solid suit of my own. If you call that strong—"

"A misfit, no solid suit of her own, and only one ace!" moaned the gentleman in the West seat. "Oh *brother!*"

"Director!" shrieked the blond lady.

The director came on the gallop, and thirty-four players looked our way from tables near and far.

"Mr. Director," rasped the lady, "will you kindly look at our opponents' announcement of system, and then inspect the North hand."

The director complied. "Well?"

"He"—pointing straight at me—"opened with one heart, and *she* responded with *two* spades!"

"And why not, I'd like to know!" put in Jackie.

The erstwhile declarer kept her cerise face toward the

director. "Naturally, I bid three clubs over two spades. Who wouldn't? If it was a weak bid, I'd be safe, But if I'd known North had a powerhouse, I certainly would have kept quiet. Now what, may I ask, are you going to do about this?"

"I have a *very* fair suggestion," said Jackie virtuously. "We'll pretend that I just bid one spade and we'll let you bid *two* clubs. That way, we only collect an eleven-hundred penalty."

A choking sound came from the lady, bringing her partner to the rescue. He said mildly, "I don't think I like that suggestion. If my partner had been able to bid two clubs over *one* spade, he"—everyone was always pointing at me—"he would have bid two diamonds and got us off the hook."

"That's silly," Jackie said. She looked at me. "You wouldn't have made such a stupid bid, would you?"

And now I was under the Klieg lights of *four* pairs of eyes.

"Darling," I said miserably, "with two infant clubs, six-five in the red suits, and no burning desire to hear a spade rebid from you—I might have bid two diamonds. It's just barely possible."

While I burned under the hot contempt in my wife's eyes, the blond lady smiled at the director. He cleared his throat. "Hmmm. Harumph, yes. I'm afraid that this is a sound protest." He gave me a commiserating look. "I'm afraid I'll have to award an adjusted score to East-West."

"Adjusted—*how?*" demanded Jackie. "This is an outrage! In case you don't know it, I happen to be a *very* old friend of Al Sobel's, and Alvin Landy's, and—"

"Darling," I said, "cease and desist. We'll take the adjusted score and like it."

"Wait!" hissed Jackie. "Just you wait!"

Bowing to right and left, clicking a figurative pair of heels, I said, "Shall we play the other board?"

The director faded away and silence reigned as we brought out the cards.

West dealer
East-West vulnerable

	NORTH	
	♠ A K Q J 7	
	♡ A 3 2	
	◇ K J 9 5 4	
	♣ —	
WEST		EAST
♠ 6 3		♠ 10 9 8 5 4 2
♡ K Q 8 7 4		♡ 6
◇ A Q 10 8		◇ 3
♣ A 8		♣ Q 6 4 3 2
	SOUTH	
	♠ —	
	♡ J 10 9 5	
	◇ 7 6 2	
	♣ K J 10 9 7 5	

West opened with one heart—and Jackie passed.

Now, I am not going to claim clairvoyance for my wife. As a matter of sober fact Jackie is not by nature a trapper; she is far too fond of bidding to go in for this technique. The truth, beyond question or doubt, is that she was simply sulking. But the result—well, to borrow a phrase from West, oh *brother!*

The auction unfolded:

West	North	East	South
1 ♡	Pass	1 ♠	Pass
2 ◇	D'ble	2 ♠	Pass
Pass	D'ble	3 ♣	D'ble
Pass	Pass	Pass	

When I reflected, late that night, that I had *toyed* with the thought of bidding three clubs over East's two spades —after Jackie put in her first double—the sweat sprang cold from my pores. To what rhetorical height (I wondered) would Jackie have soared if I had thus pulled the blond lady off the hook!

As it was, the carnage was appalling. I opened the club king, and by the time the declarer had gasped her way through the mire—quite understandably chucking a trick in her travail—she was down 1400. Again.

"This is getting to be a habit," West murmured to nobody in particular.

The blond lady placed both palms firmly on the table, and for a moment I thought she was going to do push-ups. But she managed to stand just as the director called "All change." She was still standing there, collecting her muscles, as Jackie leaned across the table and said sweetly but loudly, "We couldn't have made a slam, could we?"

Good Guessing at Bridge
A Story of an Ocean Voyage
By R. F. Foster

THREE men were lolling against the rail of an ocean greyhound that had left Queenstown that morning, bound for New York. Two of them were gamblers. They were in doubt about the third man. They had met him only once before, in the Casino at Boulogne, and had "sized him up" as a sport but had no proof of it.

They had made some advances to him there with a view to helping them to pluck a young Englishman in a game of baccarat in a private room at a hotel, but he had begged to be excused, saying that he never played anything but bridge and piquet. When asked what his racket was at those games, he declared it was simply guessing.

"I can guess what a man has almost every time," he said. "You can most always tell by the way a man's face lights up that he is crazy to make it when he is dummy in a bridge game; and in piquet, I will bet good money that I can name the deals that elder hand hasn't much show for the point."

While this struck the two experts in shuffling and shifting cuts as rather too elementary to be depended on for a livelihood, they accepted it in good faith and the three had parted on good terms. The sea being calm and the passengers having done justice to a good lunch, the three men were renewing their acquaintance and at the same time "sizing up" the passengers that walked past them with a view to forming some estimate of the crop before them and the harvest that was to come.

The bridge player, who called himself Buskirk, was very noncommittal, in spite of the efforts of the other two to draw him out by a liberal explanation of their own plans. They had marked down a wealthy Spaniard from South America and were following him up with a view to getting a good chance at him in a poker game of blind hookey. Mr. Buskirk confessed that he had no special "sucker" in view, but that he would "butt into a bridge game" if he could, as he did not care for poker.

When they asked him if he could work the cold deck in a bridge game single-handed, he smiled softly and shook his head.

"I never used a cold deck in my life. All you need in a bridge game is good guessing. If you guess the makes right oftener than the other fellows, you can win all they've got, with even cards."

"Partnership game is surer," remarked one of the others. "And an occasional no-trumper with four aces evens up the run of the cards a bit."

"But your four aces always attract attention when they show up every rubber or so. It looks bad to cut the same partner all the time, too. I can play with any of them, and pull it off if I'm guessing them good."

The conversation drifted to the passengers who were promenading the deck in the afternoon sunshine, each of them coming in for a brief and pregnant criticism from the three rail birds. After making due allowance for the deceptive nature of appearances on shipboard, the two partners estimated that there were at least a dozen who would play poker for "good money," and several who would bite on blind hookey. The bridge players were not so easy to identify.

"There is a U. S. Consul, a judge, and three doctors aboard," remarked one of the partners, pulling out a passenger list which he had carefully marked up. "That tall Englishman with the big gloves and the check trousers looks like he might be your meat, Buskirk."

"And that old fellow that walks past with his hands behind him and his head down," remarked the other, "he looks like one of those dopey duplicate-whist players who takes on bridge when he has no trays handy."

"There is no money in those think players," was Buskirk's comment. "What I watch for is to see whether a man turns out in the same suit of clothes every day. If he does, he's no good for bridge for big money. There are six men on board that have valets with them," he added, pulling out his own passenger list. "They should be pay dirt. Tomorrow, when they start the pools, will tell the story. That brings the sporting blood to the surface."

"You bet," agreed the first speaker. "I always make a note of the men that buy in their own numbers and bid for choice of high and low. They are the high rollers. No ten-cent limit game for them. Here comes something that will sit still a good bit," he continued, fastening his eye on a lame man that was toiling slowly along the deck with the aid of an ivory handled cane. He was a tall young fellow, in a covert coat, with a collar high enough to choke him, his head surmounted by a peaked cap that seemed two sizes too small for him.

Opinions were divided as to whether he would play poker or bridge, but all three agreed that he did not look particularly wealthy.

"Someone ought to tell him to chuck that cap overboard," suggested Buskirk, after he had limped past. "The fore and aft rig has been out of style for twenty years."

Next morning, the weather continuing fine, most of the passengers were out on deck and the shuffleboard fiends were at it early. Mr. Buskirk was making mental notes of the men who had changed their clothes, and turned out in new suits.

"Told you that fellow would sit still a lot," observed one of the partners, nodding toward the lame man, who was seated in a steamer chair, sucking the head of his cane and intently watching the game of shuffleboard.

"Hasn't changed his clothes either," commented the other partner. "But he sure ought to fire that steamer cap."

"The tall man that just shot is the one I hear them calling 'Judge,'" remarked Buskirk. "He looks like a dead game sport."

"Bet you the wine for dinner he plays poker instead of bridge," challenged the first speaker.

"I'll just take a guess on you," said Buskirk quietly, "and bet you the wine he does not play cards for money."

That afternoon only one small game of poker made its appearance in the smoking-room, but there were two or three bridge tables. Buskirk won his bet on the judge. Four of the men who had valets with them were bridge players. The Spaniard wanted to raise the ante at the poker table, and the lame man simply looked on, with the end of his cane in his mouth and his injured leg stretched out in front of him. He declined the invitation to join the poker party, saying the only games he knew anything of were chess and euchre. After he had gone out on the deck again for a stroll, one of the players ventured to remark that the only amusement the lame man seemed to have was sucking the head of his cane.

After the pools were sold that night, the ante at the poker table was raised to twenty-five cents, and the bridge players made it two-and-a-half. Mr. Buskirk contented himself with looking on, sitting behind a cotton broker who seemed to be a very good player, and who had a member of the Racquet Club for a partner. Between them, they proved too much for the U. S. Consul and his partner. There were the usual comments on the play by the bystanders, one of whom referred several times to his neighbor, Mr. Buskirk, but that gentleman only shook his head, declining to give any opinion on the game except that the player "didn't guess right that time."

Next morning, when the three met and compared notes while they leaned against the rail, the poker players did not seem so cheerful. There had been objections to the Spaniard's proposal to raise the limit to five dollars, and there was one man in the game who had a nasty habit of shuffling the cards when it was not his deal. Mr. Buskirk confessed that he had not been asked to play as yet, so he thought they were making the better progress.

While they were talking, the Spaniard came along and approached them with a proposal that they should have a game before lunch for five-dollar limit; just the three of them, unless their friend, Mr. Buskirk, would join?

Tempting as the opportunity was, the partners thought best to decline it, saying they wanted the air. When he had passed on they smiled at each other and wished that everyone they fished for was as hungry for the bait as that one.

The judge was taking his morning constitutional, walking at a great pace, which made still more apparent the slow progress of the lame man, who soon gave it up and dropped into a chair near the three men, stretching his neck as if his high collar was too much for him. One of the partners stepped over to help him with his rug, lifting his lame leg for him and tucking him in. When he returned to the rail he whispered to his friends:

"He's got some kind of iron brace on that game leg. Did you get on to the face he made when I touched it? He said 'thanks' about six times, but that seems to be the limit of his conversation. Doesn't seem to have much to say to anybody, and don't play cards."

"He's no good to us," remarked Buskirk, turning round and looking at the sea. "I haven't seen him buy a drink or a cigar."

The third day out it rained, and the smoking-room was uncomfortably full. Three or four poker games were in full swing and the partners had succeeded in eliminating the undesirable shuffler and had raised the limit to five dollars, at the urgent request of the Spaniard, who was quite a little ahead of the game.

The member of the Racquet Club had referred a point of play to Mr. Buskirk after being cut out of the bridge table, and had been so impressed by that gentleman's analysis of the situation and his memory of every card played that he hastened to suggest:

"Why don't you join us? We should be delighted to have you, I'm sure. Only two and a half a point, you know. The Consul wants to make it ten."

"Anything not over twenty-five suits me," replied Mr. Buskirk. "I usually quit about even any way."

Accordingly, he cut into the next rubber and the points were raised to ten cents. Buskirk cut the U. S. Consul, who got the deal. Among the spectators there was quite a little buzz of excitement when the points were raised to ten cents, and the judge, who was looking on, drew his chair closer. Everyone seemed to be either a player or a spectator at the card tables, except two who were reading, and the lame man, who was sitting in front of the open fire, gazing at it vacantly and apparently trying to swallow the head of his cane. The Englishman with the check suit and the big gloves changed his position so as to overlook the newcomer's hand.

The judge was evidently well up on bridge, for whenever he saw a play that tickled his fancy he would nudge his neighbor and smile knowingly. "I knew the Consul would take that finesse," he whispered. "Did not notice the discards. Let the bare king win a trick. Rotten play."

"The one with the black mustache that just started in looks as if he knew the game," replied the other. This allusion was to Mr. Buskirk, who, as soon as the hand was over, smiled pleasantly at the Consul, saying:

"You played that hand very nicely, partner. Did not think you could get the odd out of it," a remark which made the Englishman in the check suit look round at the others in astonishment, and caused the judge to lie back in his chair and gasp.

Some of Mr. Buskirk's makes were classified by his partner as "the limit," and he did not seem to have very good luck with them. Said he was not guessing as well as usual today. When he cut the Racquet Club man for a partner he made him a little nervous once or twice by opening short suits against no-trumpers, some of which did not work very well.

"Did not quite understand your opening, partner," the Racquet Club man explained, "but I judged it better not to return it."

"Quite right," assented Mr. Buskirk immediately. "You guessed it just right. When I open short against a no-trumper you can lead your own suit or up to dummy's weakness as you think best; but never return my lead if it is the top of nothing."

This piece of heresy made the judge exchange glances with the Englishman in the check suit and caused several other spectators to smile. A moment later their attention was attracted by a commotion at one of the poker tables, from which loud voices came. Almost everyone in the room rushed over to see what was the matter.

It appeared that the undesirable card-shuffler had been looking on and had made some remark to the Spaniard which had caused that gentleman to accuse one of the partners of cheating. This broke the ice, and several came forward to say they had known all along that the two men were gamblers. The upshot of the matter was that the game broke up, with no prospect of its being resumed with either of the two marked men in it during that voyage.

For his own protection, Mr. Buskirk thought it best to cut his two friends next morning. On meeting some of those with whom he had played bridge, he lost no time in bringing up the matter.

"Why, don't you know, I had no idea those fellows were gamblers," he began. "I had quite a talk with them on Sunday morning and I thought they were rather nice sort of chaps. But one never knows, on a steamer, when poker is the game."

Deprived of their own game, with the blind hookey proposition rendered absolutely hopeless, the two partners did not exactly see how they were going to make even their expenses on the trip, and their thoughts at once turned enviously toward the more fortunate Mr. Buskirk.

"He's making good on the bridge game, all right," remarked one to the other, "and he's got to divvy up or we'll give him away. He'll stand for a couple of hundred apiece to us, sooner than have us squeal."

Mr. Buskirk met their proposition squarely, and politely told them to "go to blazes."

"I never cheated at cards in my life," he asserted, with some warmth. "You can watch me all you like, and if you see anything crooked I'll give you every cent I've got. I don't shuffle the cards that I deal in bridge. You know that. And I deal them as square as any man living. Stand by and watch me all you want to."

"Then what's your racket?"

"I don't need any racket. I can play the game better than any of those fellows. They can't read cards. They're afraid to make it no-trumps on an ace and two queens. I'll do that every time if I feel like it, when I'm guessing good. As for ducking suits and making re-entries out of four spots—why they never heard of such things. And for guessing, they never do it. They've got rules for everything."

In spite of these protests, the two partners thought they might just as well watch the bridge game, especially as they had nothing else to do. They thought they knew enough of human nature and of gambling ethics to be pretty certain that Mr. Buskirk had some advantage or other. If it could be worked "single-handed" it was well worth learning. The great objection to bridge as a gambler's game is that one player cannot cheat at it without being caught. He must have a partner, and half the time that partner is an adversary, and what one wins the other loses.

By mutual agreement, the points had been raised to twenty-five cents at the bridge table, and everyone in the smoking-room who knew anything about the game and was not playing poker, crowded around the experts. The Englishman in the check suit was one of the first to secure a good position, and the judge took his accustomed seat, which he surrendered, however, to the lame man, who seemed to be drawn to the table by the general force of attraction. The cotton broker was just too late to get into the first rubber, but he stood close up, so that he could follow the play.

One of the disgraced poker players edged in behind Mr. Buskirk's chair, while the other stood opposite him, on the other side of the table, leaning against the chair in which the lame man sat. Both were sure that they would catch Buskirk in something or other if they watched long and closely enough, but in spite of all their knowledge of the tricks of the trade and all the sleight of hand possible with a pack of cards, neither could detect anything wrong, a conclusion which each communicated to the other by an occasional shrug and a slight lifting of the eyebrows.

The judge seemed to enjoy the play immensely, and took occasion to whisper to the lame man what he thought of some of the makes and leads. The only response he got was a regret that the cripple did not understand bridge, only euchre, after which explanation the attempts to swallow the head of the cane were resumed. With the Englishman in the check suit the judge had better luck. His commendations of the man from the Racquet Club impressed the Englishman so much that he offered to put a fiver on him to win the rubber, a bet which Mr. Buskirk, who was his adversary, declined, saying he was not "guessing them good enough" just then.

Mr. Buskirk's intimation that he was not afraid to make it no-trumps on an ace and two hopes was fully demonstrated on several occasions. One of the men who had a valet with him, and who appeared in a different suit of tweeds every day, stood close behind Mr. Buskirk for one rubber and could not help raising his eyebrows a little and glancing at his neighbor when Mr. Buskirk made it no-trumps at the score of love-all, rubber game, on the ace and five little spades, king of hearts alone, five clubs to the queen six, and one diamond.

The opening was a small heart, led from five to the ace. Dummy had two small diamonds and three small hearts, five spades to the king, ace and two small clubs. The dealer won the first trick with the king of hearts, made six tricks in spades, upon which the player on his right, who discarded from weakness, let go two clubs, keeping the ace and king of diamonds and his hearts. When the dealer led the club queen, the king covered and the jack fell, so that Mr. Buskirk made a little slam.

"That hand turned out pretty well, partner," he remarked calmly as he cut the cards for the next deal. "Of course, I guessed you had something, and I thought it better for the concealed hand to declare."

"Judging from results, you are certainly a good guesser," was the partner's comment. "If they open a diamond they make five by cards."

This hand tickled the judge so much that he tried to explain to the lame man how the discard had lost four tricks. The cripple took his cane out of his mouth and thanked him very much, regretting that he did not quite see the point, but that he believed bridge must be a very interesting game.

Some of Mr. Buskirk's opening leads were certainly calculated to excite admiration if one may measure the merit of a beginning by a successful ending. The player on his right having made it no trump, Mr. Buskirk promptly doubled, holding six clubs to the ace king, three spades to the jack and two small cards in each of the red suits.

The dealer redoubled, holding four clubs to the queen nine, three spades to the queen ten and the ace king queen of both red suits. Mr. Buskirk hesitated a moment and then redoubled, which made the well-dressed man behind him gasp. The dealer redoubled again, whereupon dummy protested and wished to avail himself of the rule permitting a player to object to doubling beyond a hundred points a trick. The dealer immediately offered to assume the responsibility and informed Mr. Buskirk that he could proceed if he wished to.

After thanking the dealer for his generosity he did redouble, and the dealer then thought he had had enough, the odd trick being worth three hundred and eighty-four points, or a hundred and ninety-two dollars to him, as he was taking both ends.

To the astonishment of both the well-dressed man and the gambler who stood beside him, Mr. Buskirk did not lead his club suit, but started with the jack of spades. Dummy laid down three small spades, five of each red suit, and no clubs. Third hand, who was the player from the Racquet Club, won the first trick with the king of spades and then stopped to do a little thinking. The judge nudged the lame man, who was falling asleep, and whispered that the leader must have made one of those rotten short-suit openings.

Finally, after due consideration of the dummy's cards, third hand returned the jack of clubs.

The dealer covered, with the queen nine and two small in his hand. Buskirk won with the king and at once led another spade. Third hand won this and led the ten of clubs without hesitation, as if the situation were now clear to him. The ten held, so he led the trey, and Buskirk's ace and seven picked up the dealer's nine and four, making four more club tricks; two by cards against the declaration.

The well-dressed man took out his handkerchief and wiped his forehead, looking round him in a dazed sort of way, as if to assure himself that it was all real. The lame man removed the cane from his mouth long enough to look up at the judge and ask quietly:

"Was that a good play then?" The judge was too astonished to answer. He was waiting for the comments of the players themselves. Mr. Buskirk was the first to speak:

"Nothing like taking a chance, partner," he remarked, breezily. "The moment he redoubled I knew he had my suit stopped and that you must come through him. Lucky guess that, though, to put you in, but it was the only suit in which I had a card that would show you I did not want the suit returned. Glad I guessed it right."

"As I remarked before, you are certainly a wonderful guesser," was the smiling comment of the Racquet Club man as he spread the cards to cut for another rubber, in which he got the cotton broker for a partner, the Consul falling to Buskirk. The Consul wanted to make it fifty cents a point; but Buskirk objected.

"Not that I am afraid of the result, partner," he said, smiling; "but I never play for more than twenty-five. We are only playing for amusement anyway, and I would just as soon play for two-and-a-half." A remark which made the two gamblers simultaneously look up at the ceiling.

Having finished dealing, Mr. Buskirk picked up his cards and found that fortune had favored him with six diamonds to the ace king queen, three very small hearts and spades and one little club. He promptly passed it, and dummy made it hearts, holding seven to the ace king jack, two small spades and four small clubs.

The adversaries made two spade tricks and the king of clubs right off the reel. The next club the dealer trumped. He discarded dummy's two remaining clubs on his own winning diamonds and then led a trump, dropping the queen and making four by cards, just enough to go game.

"Lucky I did not make it an original diamond," remarked Mr. Buskirk, cheerily. "I hate a diamond at the score of love-all, and I guessed you must have something better."

"As your former partner has remarked upon several occasions," replied the Consul, "you are a wonderful guesser."

The lame man looked up at the judge and smiled, with a gleam of intelligence in his face.

"So it's a guess game, is it? I always thought bridge was very scientific."

"All I can say," answered the judge, laughing, "is that if I could guess like that fellow I would spend the rest of my life in Wall Street."

To the end of the voyage it was the same story. Mr. Buskirk had struck his gait. Not more than once in five times did he guess wrong and not once for five minutes did he cease to be the talk of every bridge player on the boat.

Having profited to the extent of some two thousand dollars by his skill as a guesser, combined with his accurate play, Mr. Buskirk was in a liberal mood when he walked down the gangplank in New York, and he handed his less fortunate acquaintances a hundred dollars each as a consolation after they had assured him that his game was dead square.

Throwing his portmanteau, rug, and handbag into a cab he drove up to the Gilsey House, and registered, after shaking hands with the clerk.

"Billy here yet?" he inquired softly.

"Just went up to his room. Had an accident while he was away, eh? Broke his leg, or just sprained it?"

"Only a sprain. That'll be all right in a day or two. What number is he? I'll go right up and see him."

On opening the door of Billy's room, he found the

young man busy, with the assistance of the head porter, in removing a clumsy iron brace from his right leg.

After a cordial handshake Buskirk remarked:

"Billy, you did fine."

"Thanks, awfully, old man. The only thing that bothered me was when someone spoke to me, and I had to take the cane out of my mouth before I had signaled up the whole hand. The judge was a perfect nuisance that way."

"You did fine, Billy. I had to laugh at the way you kept on practising the signals with the head of your cane all day long. The only place I got stuck was when you pulled it out so far I didn't know whether my partner had the nine of clubs or the ten. But you did fine, Billy."

The Man Who Played Too Well

By Don Von Elsner

BRIDGE pro Jake Winkman stood at the window of the luxurious suite where Edna Mayberry Mallory had installed him in her imposing Tudor mansion. He fingered his black tie and frowned. There was nothing wrong with the view. It commanded a sweep of broad marble terrace and a trellised rose garden with curvacious and inviting pathways that sloped down to the lake, where gentle swells, gray-blue in the twilight, were breaking considerately against a carefully manicured beach. It always seemed a little unreal to him that the rich could contrive to have problems.

Jeanne, the Countess d'Allerez, and Prince Sergio Polensky emerged from the garden to ascend the broad marble steps of the terrace. The Prince had his arm around her and was whispering something, doubtless tender and exotically accented, into her delicate ear. Slim and seductive, the Countess was wearing a gown that featured provocatively little above the waist but billowed enticingly below. It fitted perfectly, Jake decided, into the theme of his well-chosen surroundings, but did nothing to erase his frown.

A weekend of bridge and swimming in the rarified atmosphere of conservative Lake Forest was all very well, and he had been a guest here before. The stakes would be as unrealistically high as Monopoly money; and his losses, in the improbable event that he suffered any, would be graciously absorbed by his hostess, while his winnings would be strictly between him and Internal Revenue. Not that winning would necessarily be easy. The rich, he knew, were often surprisingly adept at the game, some of them possessing an almost uncanny sense of values, while others exhibited a well-calculated dash and flair. None of them, with only a paltry few thousand at stake, was ever intimidated from backing his judgment. And he would be playing with nobility, no less. But this time it had to be different.

He had known it the moment he had answered the phone in his Hollywood apartment that morning and heard Edna's voice. "Wink, I know it's unpardonably short notice, but could you possibly catch a plane . . . this morning . . . yes, for the weekend . . . you see, my sister, Jeanne, is here . . . and a Prince Polensky . . . and Fred is away . . . Argentina, I think . . . I can't promise you anything exciting . . . but . . . I'd appreciate your coming, Wink . . ."

He had shrugged. What do you say to a woman whom you once called at three o'clock in the morning—a black and desperate morning—and asked for a million dollars—pledging whatever was left of a shopworn soul as security—and what if that woman had calmly said, "Of course, Wink . . . cash, I suppose . . . oh, dear, would eight o'clock be soon enough . . . ?" The fact that Edna

Mallory was the world's ninth richest woman—or was it eighth—was really beside the point. It was also beside the point that, as it turned out, he hadn't needed the million after all.

In the limousine from O'Hare, Edna had been her usual bland and unruffled self. Her foster sister, Jeanne, had arrived from Paris for an indefinite visit two weeks before. Instead of being pale and depressed as an aftermath of her divorce from the Count, however, she had appeared little short of radiant. True, the Count had kept her money and left her virtually penniless, but then he really needed it more because, after all, he was keeping three separate ménages in different parts of Spain. And there hadn't been any children, at least not Jeanne's. Jeanne's radiance, it seemed, stemmed from not merely one new interest, but two. One was bridge.

Jake listened resignedly. "And the other was the Prince, whom she lost little time in importing."

Edna's tone and expression remained unchanged. "Exactly. He has an even more impressive title than the Count, of course, but I think the real attraction comes from his being, of all things, a bridge expert. Jeanne asked if she might invite him, and of course I agreed.

"Oh, dear," Edna said. "Did I give a wrong impression? Forgive me. He is personable, extremely attentive, and a very fine bridge player indeed. Of course, Fred . . ."

When Fred Mallory, third, the utilities baron, had taken Edna Mayberry's hand—and her distillery millions—it had been more like a merger than a marriage. Jake wondered whether they'd had to get approval from the Justice Department.

"Spare me," he said. "I can read Fred's meter without a flashlight. But what's this about Jeanne being broke? If she's your sister, she must have got a vat full of dough—more than one lousy Count could siphon off."

"Oh, my. I do make things so difficult, don't I? You see, Jeanne was the daughter of my father's second wife. He provided quite generously for her—a million, I think—but the bulk of the estate came to me."

They were entering the hallowed confines of the world's richest community, stately trees framing an array of impressive estates. Even the air, Jake fancied, smelled different—like freshly minted money. "So she's holding her silver spoon under the spigot for another droplet or two?"

"In a way, I suppose." Edna wafted her handkerchief. She always gave the impression of being overly warm, but Jake had yet to see her really sweat. "You see, after the divorce, Fred helped me set up a trust fund for her with an ample income, but we didn't feel—Fred didn't feel . . ."

"Like kicking in with the candle-power to light up three more ménages in Spain?" He paused. "Edna, did Fred ask you to call me in—like the adjustment department—to win back the money he blew playing against Jeanne and the Prince, and before he throws the master switch?"

"Of course not, Wink. It's true, we did lose a little—about thirty-five thousand, I think. But then, Fred and I always play wretchedly together. Besides, I take care of all expenses connected with bridge."

They had turned through an imposing gateway and were cruising along a curving driveway through what appeared to be a public park—minus the public. "I gather that Jeanne and the Prince like to play set. Who made up the fourth after Fred pulled the pin?"

"Our neighbor, Randy Maxwell. You know Randy.

We played the last four nights. We lost—altogether, I think—about twenty-five thousand. Not over thirty."

Randy Maxwell was an electronics engineer who had snowballed a few patents and a gift for finance into a mountain of gold. A widower in his early fifties, Randy now piddled around the house in a three-million-dollar workshop and read books on philosophy. But Jake knew him for a keen and competent bridge player.

Fred Mallory was something else; a strict hatchet man at the bridge table, but the hatchet only worked one way —North and South. Yet each, playing with Edna, had lost about the same amount. The Prince, he decided, must be a hell of a bridge player.

He put a firm but tender hand on Edna's arm as the car drew up to the front door. "Edna, did you call me from California just to check on whether your game was slipping?" He did not mention that he had canceled a lecture and run out on two new clients in order to come.

She was looking straight ahead. "I realize it was selfish of me, Wink. I—just wanted to make sure. You're the only one . . ."

He looked at her, this middle-aged, bovine-faced woman with her potato-sack shape, and wondered whether any passion could transcend the fondness and admiration he felt toward her. She could have bought and refurbished a destroyer for a private yacht and filled it with the sycophants of her choice, people who would toady and grovel twenty-four hours a day to assure her that she was both beautiful and brilliant, or even—God forbid—sexy. Instead she chose to spend a fortune traveling month after month to major bridge tournaments, subjecting herself to the rigors of the pasteboard jungle and the grueling discipline of crossing swords with the sharpest wits in the kingdom of competitive sports. She paid the price in blood and guts and paid it like a lady because, deep down, it was more important to her to be a "do-er" than a mere "be-er."

With the footman holding the door and staring stonily, he leaned over and kissed her . . .

At dinner the Prince orchestrated the table talk like a maestro, remarking on how he had followed Winkman's exploits for years, both at and away from the bridge table, and scattering the names of European bridge luminaries like a flower girl as he tripped from chalet to château with a sprinkling of discreetly spiced anecdotes. Clearly outgunned, Jake took a leaf from Edna's book, and went quietly. The famous Winkman wit, he knew, was chiefly notable for its backfires, and he sensed an undercurrent that was already combustible enough. He patted Edna's plump knee under the table to express solidarity among the minority, and they repaired to the card room for liqueurs.

After two hours Jake was convinced that Edna was not fighting a slump, and the idea that her game might have slipped he had considered ridiculous from the first. She had been his client for more than a dozen years—second oldest to Doc McCreedy—and her game was still growing, maturing, becoming stronger both technically and tactically. *But had she thought so?* With Edna you could never tell. They had won two small rubbers and lost a larger, slowly played one, and her errors, judged analytically, were minimal. She went down on a small slam that could have been made, but Jake, following the fall of the cards, endorsed her misguess.

"Oh, dear," Edna said. "I was afraid I should have taken a different view. I just can't seem to bring home the close ones."

"Pretty hard," Jake shrugged. "So far the defense

around here has operated like its legs were crossed and wired."

It was true. From the moment the cards were dealt, the Prince had put away his cultured pearls of patter and begun to play with an almost mechanized concentration. Moreover, his game was strictly engineered for high-stake rubber bridge, a style often difficult for the match-point tournament oriented player to adjust to. His bidding was both daring and disruptive, pushing distributional hands unconscionably; while on defense he keyed solely upon defeating the contract. In high-class tournament competition his style would have earned a reputation for unreliable and erratic bidding, imprecise defense, and fetched him below average results. But he had coached the Countess well and they made a formidable combination where the payoff was in big swings. Nevertheless, when the session ended Jake and Edna had a small but tidy plus.

"Oh, dear," Edna said, meticulously dating the score sheet and passing it to the Prince and Jeanne for their initials. "It was such a pleasant session, wasn't it? I'm sure we all thoroughly enjoyed it."

The Countess, relieved of her quiet intentness, yawned prettily, and stretched. The moment was perilous, but her bodice held together. There was a faintly calculating glint in her eye as she stood up and tucked her arm under Jake's.

"I'm only sorry," she said, "I didn't take Edna up on those lessons from you long ago." She squeezed his arm and emphasized it with a little pressure from her thigh as they moved toward the stairs. Her manner was obvious enough even to put a crack in the Prince's faultless façade, particularly when she stood aside and insisted that the Prince and Edna precede them up the stairs.

Jake, whose reputation with the fair sex was considered by many to exceed even his prowess at the bridge table, recognized that he was being operated upon, but was unclear as to just how extensive a program the Countess might have in mind. He returned the pressure to let her know the game was on, and prepared to await developments, the Prince's darkly clouded face notwithstanding. He didn't think he'd overdone it, but the Countess lost her balance slightly, causing him to glance down. Stepping from tread to tread revealed her slippers beneath her floor-length gown. To his surprise, they were neither needle-heeled nor next-to-nothing sandals, but quite substantial affairs with sensible Cuban heels.

She covered the moment with a gay little laugh. "I'm afraid my balance is a trifle off, Jake. Fallen arches. My doctor in Paris has me taking special exercises and even insists on my wearing clumsy shoes. Swimming tomorrow? Elevenish?"

"That should do it," Jake said, eyes narrowed thoughtfully. "I ought to be braced for you in a bikini by then."

The next day, however, brought one of those quick changes in weather for which the Windy City and its suburbs are noted. Thunderstorms and a stiff breeze and angry whitecapped rollers invading the beach, and Winkman passed the morning losing a few dollars to Polensky at billiards. Jeanne appeared for lunch wearing an avocado sweater, cerise stretch pants, and dark green boots, while Edna wore a handcrafted holomu that looked like a hand-me-down from the washerwoman. Jake could feel the impact like a thud in the brisket, but Edna seemed unaware of the beating she was taking on the fashion front. Luncheon over, they turned as one to the card room.

During the first rubber, while Jake was continuing his

appraisal of the Prince's game, Edna pulled to a five club contract—when three no trump was cold.

NORTH (Jake)
♠ 10 3 2
♡ A K 3
◇ Q 10 7 3
♣ 10 8 4

WEST (Countess)
♠ Q 7 6 5
♡ Q 9 8
◇ A 8 5 4
♣ 9 7

EAST (Prince)
♠ K 9 8
♡ J 10 6 4
◇ K 9 6 2
♣ 5 4

SOUTH (Edna)
♠ A J 4
♡ 7 5 2
◇ J
♣ A K Q J 6 2

Jeanne led the spade five, Edna capturing the king with the ace to lead the ace and a small club to dummy's ten. She then made the only play which would give her a chance for the contract—a small diamond—and one that would have prevailed far more often than not. The Prince took his time and then produced the killing play—up with the king. When Edna later tried a ruffing finesse with the diamond queen to dispose of her losing heart, Jeanne produced the diamond ace for a one-trick set.

"I'm terribly sorry, Wink. I shouldn't have pulled."

He shrugged. "Polensky just pulled another devastater on you. We still get the hundred honors."

The Prince's eyes flashed. "Thank you, but it was

elementary. If Mrs. Mallory had the ace of diamonds the hand was cold. I had nothing to lose."

Jake let it pass. The world was full of bad analyses, including, sadly, many of his own. But switch the singleton jack of diamonds for the singleton ace, and give Jeanne the spade jack for the seven, and the Prince's play would have looked pretty silly.

But there was no denying the effectiveness of his dashing style. He and Jeanne hit a small slam that was cold but hard to reach, and followed it up with a grand slam that was tighter than an actor's girdle. But it wiped out Winkman's winnings and put the icing on the session. They abandoned the table for cocktails and then went upstairs to change for dinner.

The evening session got underway with Jeanne, ravishing in another floor-length creation, producing an unexpected defense.

	North (Edna)	
	♠ 9 5 4	
	♡ 7 6 3	
	◇ A K J 6 5	
	♣ 5 4	
West (Countess)		East (Prince)
♠ 10 7 6 3 2		♠ K Q 8
♡ K Q J 10 8		♡ 9
◇		◇ Q 10 9 8 4
♣ 9 3 2		♣ J 10 8 7
	South (Jake)	
	♠ A J	
	♡ A 5 4 2	
	◇ 7 3 2	
	♣ A K Q 6	

Jake opened with a club, over which Jeanne bid a Michaels two clubs, showing a weakish hand length in the majors. Edna called two diamonds, and Jake reached for three no trump, promptly doubled by the Prince.

Jeanne led the heart king, which held, and continued with the queen, taken by Jake, the Prince discarding the diamond four. This play virtually marked Polensky with five diamonds, and Jake's lead to the diamond king confirmed the situation when Jeanne showed out. Jake then cashed three rounds of clubs, and when Jeanne followed to all of them, he had a pretty solid inferential count on both defenders' hands—West 5–5–0–3, East 3–1–5–4. He judged further that the Prince might well have a spade trick, as well as minor suit stoppers, for his double. If so, the forceps were in position for a suicide squeeze, and he threw Jeanne in with a heart. She promptly cashed another heart, the Prince discarding first the spade eight and then the diamond nine, to bring about this position:

	North	
	♠ 9	
	♡	
	◇ A J 6 5	
	♣	
West		East
♠ 10 7 6 3		♠ K Q
♡ 8		♡ . . . .
◇		◇ Q 10
♣		♣ J
	South	
	♠ A J	
	♡	
	◇ 7 3	
	♣ 6	

If Jeanne now cashed her last heart—as Jake confidently expected—the Prince would be ground in the teeth of a progressive squeeze. But after looking long and wistfully at her good heart, the Countess reluctantly led a spade, and there was no way to keep Polensky from taking two tricks.

The Prince dabbed a handkerchief to his forehead. "Pretty play, *petite*."

"I've had it done to me before," Jake sighed. "By someone like Sheinwold and Kaplan. But one of you is better looking, and the other makes it literally royal."

Jeanne laughed gaily, but as one close contract after another fell to a withering defense, and as she and the Prince piled up the score, she finally turned to Edna. "I'm really sorry, dear sister. I know how you must feel—when you take your game so seriously."

"On the contrary," Edna responded easily. "I can't remember when I've enjoyed myself so much. Wink has proved a marvelous catalyst. Your and the Prince's game has grown so much stronger since he came. It's become almost exquisitely relentless." She sighed and waved her handkerchief. "I do hope I'm learning something."

The Prince was nimble. "Mrs. Mallory is too modest much. Your game superb is. We have been very lucky. It is of a certainty that about our cards complain we cannot."

Jake bit down on his tongue. This savored of the patronizing pap used to console pigeons in a high-stake game where they did not belong. He had spotted far too many flaws in the Prince's game to warrant any such condescension toward Edna. "Is it possible but," he asked dryly, "to deal while one the manure spreads? I have the feeling that our luck about may later turn."

And turn it did, but only for the worse. It seemed as if the Prince, resenting Jake's drollery, had determined to turn it on in earnest. The cards cooperated, and Jake and Edna took a merciless flogging. But Jake, as with almost everything else, had a technique for dealing with such situations. Having ruthlessly exorcised all superstition, he knew that judgment could be a chemical fugitive, and that once depression replaces perception at the bridge table, the victim will be contributing far more to his beating than the opponents. His answer was to forget the score, wipe out all previous hands, and to concentrate on each new hand as a fresh and isolated problem. And shuffle the hell out of the cards. He did not say it was easy, and he was grateful that Edna had learned the lesson well. Her stability in the face of repeated debacles allowed him to keep his analytical searchlight cool and probing.

NORTH (Polensky)
♠ A Q 7 3
♡ K 8 4
◇ 10 7 2
♣ 10 9 7

WEST (Edna)
♠ J 9 8 4
♡ 10 7 6 3 2
◇ A 3
♣ 6 5

EAST (Jake)
♠ 10 6
♡ A 9
◇ K J 9 8 4
♣ J 4 3 2

SOUTH (Jeanne)
♠ K 5 2
♡ Q J 5
◇ Q 6 5
♣ A K Q 8

Against Jeanne's three no trump, Edna opened the heart trey. Jake was up with the ace and switched to the diamond jack, Jeanne making a well-guessed duck. He continued the diamond nine, Edna taking her ace and exiting with the heart deuce. This was technically correct but strategically dubious, since it gave declarer too good a count on the hand. For Edna was now marked with five hearts and two diamonds. Her black cards, as well as her partner's, would almost surely break 4–2 or 3–3. If the latter, declarer had the rest; if the former, and Edna held four spades, the contract was a latch.

Jeanne won in her hand and rapidly played the spade king, followed by the ace and the king of clubs, playing dummy's seven and nine. Eyes bland, Jake now inwardly relaxed. The hand could still be made, of course, by cashing dummy's top spades, and leading a fourth spade to squeeze Winkman on Edna's forced heart return. But a player who would fail to unblock the club ten-nine for a simple proved finesse was not about to find the more intricate and unnecessary play. She didn't and struggled to a one-trick set. Cashing dummy's top spades would have ruled out Edna's holding a third club.

The Prince was gentle. "So fast, *chérie*, you play. Two different ways but you could have made the hand. Unblock the clubs or save the heart entry your hand to."

Jake said nothing, but he noted the Prince underbid the next hand the Countess played, settling for a comfortable four hearts when six was there for the price of a little skillful manipulation. But the Prince, too, was having his problems.

NORTH (Jeanne)
♠ K 7 5 2
♡ K Q 8 6
◇ Q 10 7 3
♣ 3

WEST (Jake)
♠ Q J 4
♡ A 10 9 7
◇ 8 6
♣ J 10 8 4

EAST (Edna)
♠ A 9 8
♡ . . . .
◇ 9 5 4 2
♣ Q 9 7 6 5 2

SOUTH (Prince)
♠ 10 6 3
♡ J 5 4 3 2
◇ A K J
♣ A K

Against four hearts, Jake led the spade queen, ducked in dummy by the Prince, Edna following with the nine. Since this marked declarer with the spade ten, Jake switched to the jack of clubs. Polensky won and immediately shot a low heart toward the board, Jake calmly playing the seven. When Edna showed out, the jig was up and another ice-cold contract went down the drain. Even one of Jake's beginner clients would have been sitting on toothmarks for a month, had he made such an error.

"Tough luck, partner," Jeanne consoled, thus marking herself as either a diplomat or a dolt. "All four trumps in one hand . . ."

But the Prince, enjoying belated hindsight, knew better. Had all four trumps been in the East hand, nothing could prevent the loss of two trump tricks. Therefore, it could cost nothing to insure against their all being in the *West* hand by simply leading the jack.

It was food for thought. Were the opponents exhausted from wielding the lash, or grown careless with a surfeit of loot? Winkman did not think so. Rather it seemed that the Prince was smoldering over Jeanne's continued rapid but ragged dummy play. If so, it must really have been bugging him, because on the last deal he gave an almost shocking exhibition of ineptness.

West (Jake)	North (Countess)	East (Edna)
	♠ 8 6	
	♡ 9 7 5	
	◇ A Q 5 2	
	♣ A Q 7 2	
♠ Q 4 3 2		♠ 7 5
♡ A K 10 6 3		♡ Q 8 4 2
◇ 8 6		◇ 9 4 3
♣ K 5		♣ 9 8 6 4
	South (Prince)	
	♠ A K J 10 9	
	♡ J	
	◇ K J 10 7	
	♣ J 10 3	

Against four spades, Jake led the heart king, Edna playing the eight. He continued with the ace, Polensky trumping. The Prince now carefully laid down the spade king and then entered dummy with a diamond to take a spade finesse on the way back. This sequence was like something from the fortieth of a cent game in the back room at the Y.W. Jake accepted the trick and played a third heart to Edna's queen. The Prince, down to two trumps, was now in trouble. He frowned and discarded a club, but this feeble maneuver was much too little and too late. Edna stoically produced a fourth heart and another cast-iron contract bit the dust.

As the cards lay, almost any line of play would have worked—except the one chosen by the Prince. Many rubber bridge players would simply cash the ace-king of spades, abandoning trumps if the queen failed to appear, and run the diamonds, conceding two trump tricks but bringing the hand home on the club finesse. Others might have tested the club finesse first, and then "adjusted" their view of how to play the trumps, according to whether the club play won or lost. A slightly more elegant line would be to enter dummy at trick three for an immediate trump finesse—a line that could prevail with the trump queen four deep in the East and the club king off-side—and would leave the spade eight to cover the fourth heart if it lost, and again reduce the hand to the club finesse. It was all very perplexing.

Nevertheless, the session broke up with Jake and Edna minus $38,000, give or take a few hundred.

Jake slept late. The sun was high when, clad in swim trunks and white terry cloth robe, he descended to the terrace, where a sumptuous buffet brunch awaited him. The Countess was breath-catching in a turquoise bikini with a transparent cover-up that achieved the near-ultimate in futility. The Prince was sartorially resplendent in a tailored robe of bronze and purple with a coat of arms over the left breast. As he turned to accompany Jeanne down to the sand, Jake half-expected to see POLENSKY stenciled across the back. He even sported custom-built beach sandals. When they were out of earshot, Edna turned to Jake.

"Oh, dear," she said. "I know my game is plodding and uninspired, Wink. But I feel so outclassed. And Jeanne is little more than a beginner. Perhaps I should start all over. What do you think?"

He dispatched the last of his eggs Benedict and poured himself another cup of coffee. He was deft enough at tampering with the truth, but, with Edna, there was hardly ever any need. Inside her doughy exterior, Edna had a lovely core of toughness that he had seen often bent but never broken. But he could sense that she was uniquely vulnerable now and that the breaking point was perilously close. Was that why, without quite knowing it herself, she had sent for him? He mentally riffled through his file of clichés, but after a dozen years of coaching her under the stress of tournament pressure, there was very little he had left to say.

He put down his coffee cup. "Your game is not the greatest, Edna. Maybe someday it will be. But it has integrity and it's always around the target." He paused, groping. "Bridge and golf are very similar disciplines, Edna." Edna in her culottes would never make the cover of *Vogue*, but she was a steady and competent performer on the links. "Horton Smith was a great golfer in the Hagen era, and, like most pros, a deadly putter. The press, always seeking the sensational, gave rise to the belief that Smith won tournaments because he knocked the ball in the cup from anywhere on the green. Once asked the secret of great putting, he gave a simple unsensational answer. 'The guy who sinks the most putts,' he said, 'is the guy who's closest to the pin.' Remember that, Edna."

Jake strolled down to the beach and caught the Prince

emerging from the surf. Polensky made a business of arranging his beach towel, but there was a moment when he stood barefoot, erect, and quite close. Jake slid his eyes to the horizon and back to make sure. The Prince's eyes were a good two inches below his own.

"Where's the beautiful Countess?" he asked.

"Along the bitch she swims and then back walks to exercise her feet," the Prince volunteered, quickly dropping onto his towel.

Jeanne appeared around an abutment that shielded the private beach and walked toward them along the hard-surfaced shore just above the wave-line. "Hi, champ!" she called to Winkman, accentuating a trifle the sway of her hips. "Say," she added, coming closer, "you look like an Olympics champion instead of a bridge expert."

"But which Olympics?" Jake sighed. "Anyway, it's an illusion. We have so many in our culture, don't we?"

She laughed. "Is this a new game? Find the hidden stiletto in that remark?"

He shrugged. "My stilettos are never too hard to find, Countess. Just check the nearest bull's-eye."

He left her biting a pensive lip and walked out into the surf. As a Midwestern boy, he knew the coldness of the water in the Great Lakes, but years of sheltered living around tepid pools had softened him unmercifully. He had to clench his teeth to keep going, and total immersion rivaled the ecstasy of crawling into a casket of ice. But after a dozen strokes or so, he began actually to enjoy it. It was so brutally elemental, it gave one a sense of conquest to survive. He turned and began to sidestroke his way along parallel to the beach. It was in such repetitive and mechanical activities that he often did his best thinking.

Cheating, of course, was always a thing to be considered. But to attempt to cheat against him would have required a rather massive ego. In his time he had been retained by transatlantic cruise ships, various old line clubs, private blue-book clients, and even by operators of back room cigar store games. Regardless of the site, the means were always limited, and he could almost check them off in his sleep. The adept dealer, the marked cards, the cold deck, the sloppy shuffler, the one-at-a-time-card-picker-upper. Then there were the tired old mechanical props that every bridge pro knows by heart. The tinted glasses, the hearing aid, contact lenses, the motorized wheelchair, the electronic cane, the peephole, the colleague with the binoculars, the hole in the ceiling, the taps from the floor below. Moreover, he was certain that Edna, in her bland and simplistic way, had managed to inform her guests of Winkman's familiarity with this sordid side of card life. It all made for a nice problem. Keeping the solution equally genteel might not be so easy. But he thought again of that sweat-racked night, when with no other place to turn and with a man's life in the balance, he had turned to Edna . . .

He was becoming numb. He had heard that people had frozen to death that way, in a sort of tranquil euphoria, and switched to vigorous overhand stroke, heading directly for the beach. He came ashore at a private beach two estates to the north of the Mallory's. It was deserted and he was plodding along, heading back, when a cheery voice called to him.

Jake recognized it at once as coming from Randy Maxwell. He turned to see the financier beckoning to him. Maxwell was attired in disreputable shorts and a stained T-shirt and was standing at the entrance to what appeared to be a well-tended jungle.

Jake joined him and saw that the trees concealed a squat functional building of concrete and hollow tile.

"My hobby shop," Randy explained. "Since the word 'work' is vulgarly *de trop* around here, I had to draw it up as a 'summer house' to get a building permit—and then hide it."

Inside, even Jake's unsophisticated eye could detect a few hundred thousand dollars' worth of electronic toys. "What do you do in here?" he asked. "Besides compute relative strength indices on the Dow-Jones averages."

Randy laughed. "Believe it or not, I've got a computer that does just that. Mainly, I piddle. What I'm really trying to do, I suppose, is recapture what I had in my garage down on South Sangamon Street twenty-five years ago. I used to piddle with impractical, noncommercial things, and one year I made twelve million. Now, of course, such things are done in what is called a laboratory, and it's considered unseemly for me to be caught in one. I pay young squirts fabulous salaries to do what I'd cheerfully do for nothing." He pointed to the array of equipment. "But it isn't the same. I just don't get the ideas anymore."

"Even the Greeks didn't have a word for it," Jake said. "Slip me another Polaroid, and I'll sit down and weep with you, Alexander."

Maxwell shook his head. "It would spoil you, Jake. I wouldn't want to be a party to that. Integrity is fine, but it's twice as fine when it costs till it hurts." He turned cheerful again. "Here." He handed Jake two plastic boxes about the size of match boxes. "Let's try something."

"Behind you and to your left," Randy went on, "there's a cabinet with a shelf full of large capacitors."

"What's a capacitor?"

"A radio-electronic device. There are also some small condensers."

"Same question."

"Same answer. I am going to tell you how many of each. Listen closely."

Suddenly Jake became aware of a soundless tingling in his left hand and recognized a series of six impulses. Then came a series of shorter or lighter impulses. "Six capacitors and ten condensers," he said. "The last time I was in your house you had a bottle of Scotch that talked in a whiskey tenor. I liked that trick better."

"Me, too," Randy said. "But we have to be practical."

"Indeed. And what will this thing do? Communicate with your refrigerator to give you different colored ice cubes?"

"It is one of the world's great myths, Jake, that real progress comes from creating to fill a need. Such efforts are always stodgy and pedestrian. Create first; find the need later. Check that cabinet."

Jake checked and found the six capacitors and ten condensers.

"Now move a number of condensers down to the next shelf and tell me how many by pressing down with your right thumb."

Jake moved three, and pressed down on the black box in his right hand three times.

"Three," Randy said. "Isn't that nice? No wires, no sound." A phone rang. "Damn," he said, putting it down. "Another directors' meeting. Got to run. Stop over for a drink before you leave, Jake."

Jake resumed his stroll along the beach, coming presently to the abutment where he had first spotted Jeanne. He found himself almost treading on her small but well-formed footprints.

Edna's beach was deserted, and he gathered up his robe and headed directly for his shower. Coming out, he began carefully to pack. He worked at remaining cool and dispassionate, sipping rye and water because it seemed to him to have a clean taste. Sometimes he even brushed his teeth with it. But the sour nausea was not in his mouth or stomach. He took a deep breath, followed the broad upstairs hall to the south wing, and tapped on Jeanne's door.

The Countess was reclining on a love seat in canary yellow lounging pajamas and looked almost feverishly fetching. She sat up and gave him a warm smile. "Let me fix you a drink. What a pleasant surprise. But this is hardly the hour for a seduction, is it?"

Jake sat down across from her and accepted the drink. "I wouldn't know. I haven't gotten around to punching a time card on it."

She laughed. "You're such a devastating rebuker, Wink. Do you really enjoy cutting people up, or is it just a pose?"

"In this case, neither," Jake said. "It's a job. Something like swabbing down the head—somebody has to do it. It'll help if we omit the headshrinker jargon about sibling hostilities. You and Edna were raised as sisters, but you have everything and she's a dowdy frump. You glitter and sparkle and have royal consorts, and all she can do is blink her bovine eyes. Of course, it's unbelievably cruel that she should have the money instead of you. But I don't think money is the whole story, Jeanne. You could marry a bundle. It's got to be something else. Edna's got something that infuriates you. It completely distorts your perspective. You've spent years pirouetting around her, mercilessly tossing your darts, artfully searching out her most vulnerable parts. You do it with your clothes, your style, your men—you'd even toss in an affair with me, once you sensed it would wound her. But Edna won't show hurt. That's an aristocracy that you just can't comprehend. Over the years you've hit her with everything in your sick arsenal. But she won't show hurt. She just chews her cud and endures it. But suppose you could humiliate her at bridge? She couldn't pretend to ignore that, could she? And with me as her partner? The skin should really be thin and tender there, shouldn't it? But your vaulting fury overreached itself."

The Countess' face was a white mask. "Indeed? In what way?"

"You got carried away by the caprice of a few cards. You wanted the ecstasy of plunging the knife yourself. You played the dummy too fast for little Sergie to clue you. Not that he's the greatest . . ."

Her face was suddenly mottled with rage. "Why, you—you point-count gigolo. You cheap pasteboard mercenary. Don't you dare speak to me that way. Don't tell me you're really fond of the old sow! How much is she paying you? Tell me that!" She was standing over him, her bodice heaving.

Jake sipped his drink. "Edna would never pay me for a favor, Jeanne. Besides, anything I could do for her was paid for long, long ago—and not with money." He looked out the window. "I'm a creampuff as well as a dreamer, Jeanne. I can't protect Edna from all the hurts in the world, much as I might like to, but I can protect her from a pair of filthy frauds—and will."

She turned suddenly calculating. "Oh, come now. Let's not make wildly slanderous statements. Besides, Sergio—"

Jake sighed. "Sergio said we can always buy him. But you see, Countess, Sergie is sadly two inches shorter on the beach than in the drawing room."

Her eyes narrowed. "So he wears elevator shoes. What has a little male vanity got to do with anything?"

"About the same amount," Jake said, "as phony fallen

arches. Half-firm sand takes a fairly revealing footprint. You may be fallen, Countess, but the problem is not in your arches."

"Just what are you getting at?"

"Many things. None of them pretty. I suspect that against Fred and Randy all you really needed was the receiver, which you could hide in your hair, and, consequently, there was no mention of your bad arches and clumsy shoes. But when I came into the act, you had to go on two-way communication. That's why you wanted me beside you and Edna ahead of you when you went up the stairs. Is that enough? I'll deal with Sergie later."

She gave him a venomous glare. "That does it! The only thing you'll deal with later is my attorney." She grasped the top of her pajamas, ready to rip. "If you're not out of here in five seconds with your lips sealed, I'm going to scream rape!"

But Jake wasn't there to protest. "Excuse me for being rude to the crude," he said, from the region of her closet. "A topless bridge player should make a peek worth even more than two finesses. But I'm after even bigger skin game."

He returned with an armload of her shoes. Whether it was this or his remark that inhibited her, she did not scream. Several of them, he noted, were made by a custom cobbler in Florence, and had one feature in common—a nice substantial heel. A little toying revealed the clever way in which they could be detached, and the equally deft manner in which they had been hollowed. Quite enough to conceal a little black box—one in each heel. He sighed. The rich often spoke in parables. Randy Maxwell would never dream of accusing one of Edna's guests of rooking him out of thirty grand. But he'd spend a week figuring out how it was done, drop suave and subtle suggestions to Edna about importing Jake Winkman, and then contrive to get Jake to do the dirty work. But the really important task remained.

The Countess, watching him, had difficulty lighting a cigarette. She blew out a cloud of smoke. "Okay. Now what?"

"I go through the rest of your shoes and search the room until I find the transmitter and receiver—or you hand them to me."

She dug them out from behind the cushions of the love seat and handed them to him, a look of actual triumph suddenly lighting her eyes. "There. Now call Edna and explain to her how her little sister and ward abused her hospitality and cheated her. Go on. Maybe she'll prefer charges and we can make an international thing out of it."

He smiled ruefully. "No wonder you're such a lousy bridge player. Listen to me, Jeanne. I don't think you're all that bad or all that stupid. Besides, I need your help. Edna wouldn't prefer charges. She'd probably apologize for inspiring your perfidy. But she'd be hurt, and we don't really want that, do we?"

She gawked. "Are you kidding? I should cooperate with you to spare that cretin's feelings! Just how will you manage that?"

"By cutting out your heart, if I have to," Jake said. "We're going downstairs in a few minutes for a session of bridge—and just in case there's more of these around—you'll be wearing bedroom slippers."

She sat forward in rigid disbelief. "So you can cut Serg and me to pieces just to plaster up Edna's ego? And take back our hard-earned money? Do you realize how much time and effort we—Try to make me!"

"If you insist." He moved to the door. "I'll let pride put a pitchfork to your derrière. You see, Jeanne, Sergie is not a bridge expert."

"Not a bridge expert!" She actually goggled. "What do you mean? Why everyone—even Edna—has complimented him on his game. At Nice and Cannes he was always a big winner."

Jake shook his head. "He played too well," he said, "on defense. When he was practically looking at all four hands. Bridge doesn't work that way. There are a hundred fine dummy players for every topflight defensive player. He is a middling fair casino-style player—what we call a palooka-killer. Since you asked for it, brace yourself. Sergie is a con man. He promoted you for the sole purpose of getting into this house and out again—with a bundle. By involving you, he provided himself with complete immunity even if he was caught. If I know the type—and believe me I do—I'll bet he brought his mistress along when he followed you over here. He's got her stashed at some downtown hotel. Hasn't he made a quick trip or two to see his 'consulate'?"

A flash of terror mixed with betrayal lit up her eyes. "That's a lie! Serge is madly in love with me. We're going to be married. It was only because of his love for me that we needed—"

"Another fifty thousand shares of RCA. Face it, Jeanne. After our afternoon session, Serge will check with you during the dinner break. Don't tell him I've drawn his fangs. Simply say that you consider yourself a better bridge player than Edna and that, since his is better than I, why not enjoy the added sport of beating us fair and square? If you really have a sophisticated sense of humor, you'll enjoy the look that comes into his eye. But within an hour after the evening session starts, little Sergie is going to get an urgent call. His Upper Slobovian uncle, the grand duke, is dying in Zürich. Surely he has told you about the grand duke . . ."

Her mouth was like a thin fresh scar. "You are the most despicable, cynical, skeptical rat-fink I've encountered. Get out!"

The afternoon session was a subdued affair with both the Countess and the Prince playing with a withdrawn, almost desperate intentness. Edna, appearing not to notice, was nonetheless impelled to flow copious coats of lacquer to preserve a patina of social grace. The cards ran flat and indecisive, but Jake drove them, scoring game after game with the aid of a little inept defense. Three times he pushed to the five level in quest of dubious slams, but each time, failing to hold the critical controls, Edna correctly signed him off. He was almost equally relentless in presenting Edna with tough, brutally stretched contracts, but she bagged far more than her share with beautifully judged dummy play.

"Oh, dear," she observed, as the session broke up. "I seem to be so lucky today." Her eyes met Jake's blandly. "You played magnificently, Wink. It's such a pleasure, isn't it? Thank you. Shall we resume about eight? I must tell Hanson." She presented the score to Jeanne and the Prince. They were down $27,000.

Edna's performance at dinner, Jake decided, deserved at the very least an Academy Award. She was serenely solicitous, fumbled the table talk into channels that were as bland as an ulcer diet, and avoided any word or mannerism that might hint at a feeling of triumph. How much did she know? Or suspect? He'd be damned if he could tell. He thought of Kipling and of treating those two imposters—"triumph and disaster"—just the same. He was seated at her right—and that was another thing. For there were two other guests tonight—Randy Maxwell and a dowager by the name of Mrs. Adrian Phelps. Like a litany, it kept bugging him. *How much did Edna know?* He put down his coffee cup, picked up her chubby hand and kissed it . . . No one seemed to take the slightest notice, least of all Edna.

The evening session was scarcely under way before Jake and Edna smoothly assumed a comfortable margin. Maxwell and Mrs. Phelps were playing in a quiet game of Persian rummy at a nearby table. The Prince made one of his dashing bids, ran into a rock-crusher in Jake's hand, and got pulverized. Randy and Mrs. Phelps came over to observe the carnage. It was almost a relief when Hanson appeared to inform the Prince of an urgent phone call. He excused himself to take it in the library. When he returned his face was clouded.

"I am prostrated," he announced. "An unpardonable turn of events. I must at once leave. It concerns a matter about which I cannot speak." He bowed deeply and headed rapidly for the stairs. The Countess looked as if she had been drugged, but Jake noted a tiny ember smoldering in her eye.

The whole tempo went into a new gear. Many things happened fast, but there was an almost stage-like coordination about them, so that they seemed to take place with slow-motion definition. Edna withdrew to a nearby escritoire and carefully wrote a check. The Prince's bag appeared almost as if by magic in the front hall, followed by the Prince himself. He accepted Edna's check, clicked his heels, and was gone, a waiting cab whisking him away. Mrs. Phelps was in his seat at the bridge table, calmly shuffling the cards.

Randy Maxwell lit a cigar and nudged Jake toward the library. "The call came from the Uppingham Hotel on East Delaware, but it was a little cryptic," he said. He blew out a puff of smoke. "You did want me to tap the phone, didn't you?"

Jake shrugged. "What else, Steinmetz? It was probably better than bribing Hanson to listen in."

"Oh, much better," Randy agreed. "Some people are so devious." He took a small radio from his pocket. "I just happen to have this tuned to the cab company's frequency." There was a squawk . . . "thirty-seven to dispatch . . . pickup at Mallory . . . destination Pierpont Plaza . . . ten-four" . . . Maxwell pocketed the radio and turned to Jake. "You see? Perhaps we can have that drink next time."

Jake's bags had replaced the Prince's in the hall, and a Mercedes was idling under the porte cochere. "Mrs. Mallory ordered it brought around when she saw your bags," Hanson said.

"I daresay you'll leave it at the airport, sir?"

Jake nodded. "I'd rather not disturb Mrs. Mallory just now. Say good-bye for me when she's free. In fact, give her a kiss for me, Hanson."

"Only you could do that, sir. You're the only one I've ever seen—I think I may have said too much, sir."

Jeanne was in the front seat. He whipped the car out through the long curving driveway. "You're about to get your ego shattered, Countess. Are you sure you can take it?"

"Drop the Countess stuff, Wink. I'm a skurvy, rotten nothing. I need a catharsis."

"Castor oil is cheap."

"But it won't make me into an Edna?"

"Only Edna could make Edna."

She was silent for several miles. "Wink, what do you honestly think of my bridge game?"

"With or without an electronic mirror? Without, it stinks."

"I *know* it stinks. I meant do I have the latent ability?"

"Anyone has the ability; not everyone the guts."

Nothing more was said until Jake pulled into the parking lot of the Pierpont Plaza on Chicago's near-North side. She handed him a small camera. "Randy said to give you this. It has a built-in electronic flash that will take pictures in any light."

"Polensky," Jake told the desk clerk. "Give me his room number and tell him Jake Winkman's on his way up."

The Prince was completely urbane. So was the bleached blonde with the long cigarette holder who lounged on the divan. "It was thoughtful of you to spare Mrs. Mallory the scene," he said. "But you have had a trip for nothing." He completely ignored Jeanne. "Mrs. Mallory will not make the charge. Nor Mr. Maxwell. Nor will she stop the check." He shrugged his shoulders. "So there is to discuss really nothing."

"True," Jake admitted. He unstrapped one of the Prince's bags, sprawling the contents on the floor, and came up with a shoe. He calmly detached a heel, placed shoe and heel on an end table, and proceeded to photograph them.

The Prince suddenly changed to a tiger, showing his fangs in the form of a small automatic. "Give me that camera. I demand also payment for my ruined shoe. Then get out or I will shoot!"

Jake snapped his picture. "Sergie, you are many things, but a gunman isn't one of them. Besides, Mr. Maxwell doesn't trust me. I spotted two detectives from the Bronco squad in the lobby." He snapped a picture of the blonde. "Be a good fellow and give me the check."

The tiger turned to a fawning jackal. "But that I cannot. I have the expenses." His eyes slithered to the blonde. "Very heavy expenses. And I need money Europe to return." He spread his arms. "Let us like gentlemen the compromise make."

The blonde began to pack. It didn't take her long.

Winkman shook his head. "These pictures and a full report will go to the American Contract Bridge League and the World Bridge Federation. You'll be blown from Oslo to Oskaloosa, right down to your denture charts. You've had it, Sergie. The check."

The blonde hustled her bags to the door. "Serg, you always were a yellow fink. The man says two words and you curl up like wet spaghetti. He hasn't a thing on you that would stand up. You could sue and double your money on a settlement. Mrs. Mallory would no more let this come out in court than fly. Her own sister . . . The least you could do is beat this man up and throw him out. Good-bye!" She slammed the door.

The Prince was nervously lighting a cigarette. He flung it down in a sudden gesture of ultimate frustration and made a desperate lunge at Winkman. At the last second, Jake stepped aside and measured him for a Judo sweep that scythed his legs from under him and dropped him like a bag of wet cement. He leaned down and retrieved Edna's check from the Prince's wallet. Maxwell's check was missing, but there was $20,000 in large denomination bills with the bank's paper strap still around them.

He held out his hand to Jeanne. "Give me your lighter."

White-faced, she handed it to him and he touched the flame to the check.

Three more times on the way to the airport, he asked to borrow her lighter.

"That—that woman," Jeanne said, as they pulled into O'Hare. "She was right, wasn't she? You just psyched him."

He looked at her and sadly shook his head. "Let's just say I seldom psych."

She sat up as if suddenly galvanized. "Good heavens! Do you actually believe that Edna might have done it? Reveal herself and the great Fred Mallory as dupes and unwitting shills—and her own sister as a crook! Do you honestly think—"

"I don't know," Jake said softly. "Edna's a quality person. I suspect she'd choose the integrity that cost her the most. I'm glad it won't be necessary. Lighter, please."

She was silent as he slid out of the car, gathered his grips, and handed her the envelope with the $20,000 for Randy Maxwell. "Jake . . . wait. Why have you kept borrowing my lighter? What happened to that beautiful gold lighter that Edna gave you?"

"It's in Sergie's pocket with his fingerprints all over it. I put it there when he went to answer the phone. If he'd made a fuss—as his mistress suggested—I'd have nailed him on grand larceny. And don't kid yourself I wouldn't have pressed the charge."

She sat looking up at him for a long moment. "For a dumpy, frumpy woman like Edna?"

"No," he said. "Just for Edna."

In the rotunda, he picked up a public phone, and got Edna.

"I think Jeanne is coming home," he said. He hoped he had got the right inflection on the word "home." But with Edna you could never tell.

"Thank you, Wink, we're waiting. It's been such a pleasant day, hasn't it?"

The Three Fat Women of Antibes

By W. Somerset Maugham

ONE was called Mrs. Richman and she was a widow. The second was called Mrs. Sutcliffe; she was American and she had divorced two husbands. The third was called Miss Hickson and she was a spinster. They were all in the comfortable forties and they were all well off. Mrs. Sutcliffe had the odd first name of Arrow. When she was young and slender she had liked it well enough. It suited her, and the jests it occasioned, though too often repeated, were very flattering; she was not disinclined to believe that it suited her character too: it suggested directness, speed and purpose. She liked it less now that her delicate features had grown muzzy with fat, that her arms and shoulders were so substantial and her hips so massive. It was increasingly difficult to find dresses to make her look as she liked to look. The jests her name gave rise to now were made behind her back, and she very well knew that they were far from obliging. But she was by no means resigned to middle age. She still wore blue to bring out the colour of her eyes and, with the help of art, her fair hair had kept its lustre. What she liked about Beatrice Richman and Frances Hickson was that they were both so much fatter than she, it made her look quite slim; they were both of them older and much inclined to treat her as a little young thing. It was not disagreeable. They were good-natured women, and they chaffed her pleasantly about her beaux; they had both given up the thought of that kind of nonsense, indeed Miss Hickson had never given it a moment's consideration, but they were sympathetic to her flirtations. It was understood that one of these days Arrow would make a third man happy.

"Only you mustn't get any heavier, darling," said Mrs. Richman.

"And for goodness' sake make certain of his bridge," said Miss Hickson.

They saw for her a man of about fifty, but well preserved and of distinguished carriage, an admiral on the retired list and a good golfer, or a widower without encumbrances, but in any case with a substantial income. Arrow listened to them amiably, and kept to herself the fact that this was not at all her idea. It was true that she would have liked to marry again, but her fancy turned to a dark slim Italian with flashing eyes and a sonorous title or to a Spanish don of noble lineage; and not a day more than thirty. There were times when, looking at herself in her mirror, she was certain she did not look any more than that herself.

They were great friends, Miss Hickson, Mrs. Richman and Arrow Sutcliffe. It was their fat that had brought them together and bridge that had cemented their alliance. They had met first at Carlsbad, where they were staying at the same hotel and were treated by the same doctor who used them with the same ruthlessness. Beatrice Richman was enormous. She was a handsome woman, with fine eyes, rouged cheeks and painted lips.

She was very well content to be a widow with a handsome fortune. She adored her food. She liked bread and butter, cream, potatoes and suet puddings, and for eleven months of the year ate pretty well everything she had a mind to, and for one month went to Carlsbad to reduce. But every year she grew fatter. She upbraided the doctor, but got no sympathy from him. He pointed out to her various plain and simple facts.

"But if I'm never to eat a thing I like life isn't worth living," she expostulated.

He shrugged his disapproving shoulders. Afterwards she told Miss Hickson that she was beginning to suspect he wasn't so clever as she had thought. Miss Hickson gave a great guffaw. She was that sort of woman. She had a deep bass voice, a large flat sallow face from which twinkled little bright eyes; she walked with a slouch, her hands in her pockets, and when she could do so without exciting attention smoked a long cigar. She dressed as like a man as she could.

"What the deuce should I look like in frills and furbelows?" she said. "When you're as fat as I am you may just as well be comfortable."

She wore tweeds and heavy boots and whenever she could went about bareheaded. But she was as strong as an ox and boasted that few men could drive a longer ball than she. She was plain of speech, and she could swear more variously than a stevedore. Though her name was Frances she preferred to be called Frank. Masterful, but with tact, it was her jovial strength of character that held the three together. They drank their waters together, had their baths at the same hour, they took their strenuous walks together, pounded about the tennis court with a professional to make them run, and ate at the same table their sparse and regulated meals. Nothing impaired their good humour but the scales, and when one or other of them weighed as much on one day as she had the day before neither Frank's coarse jokes, the *bonhomie* of Beatrice nor Arrow's pretty kittenish ways sufficed to dispel the gloom. Then drastic measures were resorted to, the culprit went to bed for twenty-four hours and nothing passed her lips but the doctor's famous vegetable soup which tasted like hot water in which a cabbage had been well rinsed.

Never were three women greater friends. They would have been independent of anyone else if they had not needed a fourth at bridge. They were fierce, enthusiastic players, and the moment the day's cure was over they sat down at the bridge table. Arrow, feminine as she was, played the best game of the three, a hard, brilliant game, in which she showed no mercy and never conceded a point or failed to take advantage of a mistake. Beatrice was solid and reliable. Frank was dashing; she was a great theorist, and had all the authorities at the tip of her tongue. They had long arguments over the rival systems. They bombarded one another with Culbertson and Sims. It was obvious that not one of them ever played a card without fifteen good reasons, but it was also obvious from the subsequent conversation that there were fifteen equally good reasons why she should not have played it. Life would have been perfect, even with the prospect of twenty-four hours of that filthy soup when the doctor's rotten (Beatrice) bloody (Frank) lousy (Arrow) scales pretended one hadn't lost an ounce in two days, if only there had not been this constant difficulty of finding someone to play with them who was in their class.

It was for this reason that on the occasion with which this narrative deals Frank invited Lena Finch to come and stay with them at Antibes. They were spending some weeks there on Frank's suggestion. It seemed absurd to her, with her common sense, that immediately the cure was over Beatrice who always lost twenty pounds should by giving way to her ungovernable appetite put it all on again. Beatrice was weak. She needed a person of strong will to watch her diet. She proposed then that on leaving Carlsbad they should take a house at Antibes where they could get plenty of exercise, everyone knew that nothing slimmed you like swimming, and as far as possible could go on with the cure. With a cook of their own they could at least avoid things that were obviously fattening. There was no reason why they should not all lose several pounds more. It seemed a very good idea. Beatrice knew what was good for her, and she could resist temptation well enough if temptation was not put right under her nose. Besides, she liked gambling, and a flutter at the Casino two or three times a week would pass the time very pleasantly. Arrow adored Antibes, and she would be looking her best after a month at Carlsbad. She could just pick and choose among the young Italians, the passionate Spaniards, the gallant Frenchmen and the long-limbed English who sauntered about all day in bathing trunks and gay-coloured dressing gowns. The plan worked very well. They had a grand time. Two days a week they ate nothing but hard-boiled eggs and raw tomatoes, and they mounted the scales every morning with light hearts. Arrow got down to eleven stone and felt just like a girl; Beatrice and Frank by standing in a certain way just avoided the thirteen. The machine they had bought registered kilogrammes, and they got extraordinarily clever at translating these in the twinkling of an eye to pounds and ounces.

But the fourth at bridge continued to be the difficulty. This person played like a foot, the other was so slow that it drove you frantic, one was quarrelsome, another was a bad loser, a third was next door to a crook. It was strange how hard it was to find exactly the player you wanted.

One morning when they were sitting in pyjamas on the terrace overlooking the sea, drinking their tea (without milk or sugar) and eating a rusk prepared by Dr. Hudebert and guaranteed not to be fattening, Frank looked up from her letters.

"Lena Finch is coming down to the Riviera," she said.

"Who's she?" asked Arrow.

"She married a cousin of mine. He died a couple of months ago, and she's just recovering from a nervous breakdown. What about asking her to come here for a fortnight?"

"Does she play bridge?" asked Beatrice.

"You bet your life she does," boomed Frank in her deep voice. "And a damned good game too. We should be absolutely independent of outsiders."

"How old is she?" asked Arrow.

"Same age as I am."

"That sounds all right."

It was settled. Frank, with her usual decisiveness, stalked out as soon as she had finished her breakfast to send a wire, and three days later Lena Finch arrived. Frank met her at the station. She was in deep but not obtrusive mourning for the recent death of her husband. Frank had not seen her for two years. She kissed her warmly and took a good look at her.

"You're very thin, darling," she said.

Lena smiled bravely.

"I've been through a good deal lately. I've lost a lot of weight."

Frank sighed, but whether from sympathy with her cousin's sad loss, or from envy, was not obvious.

Lena was not, however, unduly depressed, and after a quick bath was quite ready to accompany Frank to Eden Røc. Frank introduced the stranger to her two friends and they sat down in what was known as the Monkey House. It was an enclosure covered with glass overlooking the sea, with a bar at the back, and it was crowded with chattering people in bathing costumes, pyjamas or dressing gowns, who were seated at the tables having drinks. Beatrice's soft heart went out to the lorn widow, and Arrow, seeing that she was pale, quite ordinary to look at and probably forty-eight, was prepared to like her very much. A waiter approached them.

"What will you have, Lena dear?" Frank asked.

"Oh, I don't know, what you all have, a dry Martini or a White Lady."

Arrow and Beatrice gave her a quick look. Everyone knows how fattening cocktails are.

"I daresay you're tired after your journey," said Frank kindly.

She ordered a dry Martini for Lena and a mixed lemon and orange juice for herself and her two friends.

"We find alcohol isn't very good in all this heat," she explained.

"Oh, it never affects me at all," Lena answered airily, "I like cocktails."

Arrow went very slightly pale under her rouge (neither she nor Beatrice ever wet their faces when they bathed, and they thought it absurd of Frank, a woman of her size, to pretend she liked diving), but she said nothing. The conversation was gay and easy, they all said the obvious things with gusto, and presently they strolled back to the villa for luncheon.

In each napkin were two little antifat rusks. Lena gave a bright smile as she put them by the side of her plate.

"May I have some bread?" she asked.

The grossest indecency would not have fallen on the ears of those three women with such a shock. Not one of them had eaten bread for ten years. Even Beatrice, greedy as she was, drew the line there. Frank, the good hostess, recovered herself first.

"Of course, darling," she said, and turning to the butler asked him to bring some.

"And some butter," said Lena in that pleasant easy way of hers.

There was a moment's embarrassed silence.

"I don't know if there's any in the house," said Frank, "but I'll enquire. There may be some in the kitchen."

"I adore bread and butter, don't you?" said Lena, turning to Beatrice.

Beatrice gave a sickly smile and an evasive reply. The butler brought a long crisp roll of French bread. Lena slit it in two and plastered it with the butter which was miraculously produced. A grilled sole was served.

"We eat very simply here," said Frank. "I hope you won't mind."

"Oh, no, I like my food very plain," said Lena as she took some butter and spread it over her fish. "As long as I can have bread and butter and potatoes and cream I'm quite happy."

The three friends exchanged a glance. Frank's great sallow face sagged a little, and she looked with distaste at the dry, insipid sole on her plate. Beatrice came to the rescue.

"It's such a bore, we can't get cream here," she said. "It's one of the things one has to do without on the Riviera."

"What a pity," said Lena.

The rest of the luncheon consisted of lamb cutlets, with the fat carefully removed so that Beatrice should not be led astray, and spinach boiled in water, with stewed pears to end up with. Lena tasted her pears and gave the butler a look of enquiry. That resourceful man understood her at once, and though powdered sugar had never been served at that table before, handed her without a moment's hesitation a bowl of it. She helped herself liberally. The other three pretended not to notice. Coffee was served, and Lena took three lumps of sugar in hers.

"You have a very sweet tooth," said Arrow in a tone which she struggled to keep friendly.

"We think saccharine so much more sweetening," said Frank, as she put a tiny tablet of it into her coffee.

"Disgusting stuff," said Lena.

Beatrice's mouth drooped at the corners, and she gave the lump sugar a yearning look.

"Beatrice!" boomed Frank sternly.

Beatrice stifled a sigh and reached for the saccharine.

Frank was relieved when they could sit down to the bridge table. It was plain to her that Arrow and Beatrice were upset. She wanted them to like Lena, and she was anxious that Lena should enjoy her fortnight with them. For the first rubber Arrow cut with the newcomer.

"Do you play Vanderbilt or Culbertson?" she asked her.

"I have no conventions," Lena answered in a happy-go-lucky way, "I play by the light of nature."

"I play strict Culbertson," said Arrow acidly.

The three fat women braced themselves to the fray. No conventions indeed! They'd learn her. When it came to bridge even Frank's family feeling was forgotten, and she settled down with the same determination as the others to trim the stranger in their midst. But the light of nature served Lena very well. She had a natural gift for the game and great experience. She played with imagination, quickly, boldly, and with assurance. The other players were in too high a class not to realize very soon that Lena knew what she was about, and since they were all thoroughly good-natured, generous women, they were gradually mollified. This was real bridge. They all enjoyed themselves. Arrow and Beatrice began to feel more kindly towards Lena, and Frank, noticing this, heaved a fat sigh of relief. It was going to be a success.

After a couple of hours they parted, Frank and Beatrice to have a round of golf, and Arrow to take a brisk walk with a young Prince Roccamare whose acquaintance she had lately made. He was very sweet and young and good-looking. Lena said she would rest.

They met again just before dinner.

"I hope you've been all right, Lena dear," said Frank. "I was rather conscience-stricken at leaving you with nothing to do all this time."

"Oh, don't apologize. I had a lovely sleep, and then I went down to Juan and had a cocktail. And d'you know what I discovered? You'll be so pleased. I found a dear little teashop where they've got the most beautiful thick fresh cream. I've ordered half a pint to be sent every day. I thought it would be my little contribution to the household."

Her eyes were shining. She was evidently expecting them to be delighted.

"How very kind of you," said Frank, with a look that sought to quell the indignation that she saw on the faces of her two friends. "But we never eat cream. In this climate it makes one so bilious."

"I shall have to eat it all myself then," said Lena cheerfully.

"Don't you ever think of your figure?" Arrow asked with icy deliberation.

"The doctor said I must eat."

"Did he say you must eat bread and butter and potatoes and cream?"

"Yes. That's what I thought you meant when you said you had simple food."

"You'll get simply enormous," said Beatrice.

Lena laughed gaily.

"No, I shan't. You see, nothing ever makes me fat. I've always eaten everything I wanted to, and it's never had the slightest effect on me."

The stony silence that followed this speech was only broken by the entrance of the butler.

"*Mademoiselle est servie,*" he announced.

They talked the matter over late that night, after Lena had gone to bed, in Frank's room. During the evening they had been furiously cheerful, and they had chaffed one another with a friendliness that would have taken in the keenest observer. But now they dropped the mask. Beatrice was sullen, Arrow was spiteful and Frank was unmanned.

"It's not very nice for me to sit there and see her eat all the things I particularly like," said Beatrice plaintively.

"It's not very nice for any of us," Frank snapped back.

"You should never have asked her here," said Arrow.

"How was I to know?" cried Frank.

"I can't help thinking that if she really cared for her husband she would hardly eat so much," said Beatrice. "He's only been buried two months. I mean, I think you ought to show some respect for the dead."

"Why can't she eat the same as we do?" asked Arrow viciously. "She's a guest."

"Well, you heard what she said. The doctor told her she must eat."

"Then she ought to go to a sanatorium."

"It's more than flesh and blood can stand, Frank," moaned Beatrice.

"If I can stand it you can stand it."

"She's your cousin, she's not our cousin," said Arrow. "I'm not going to sit there for fourteen days and watch that woman make a hog of herself."

"It's so vulgar to attach all this importance to food," Frank boomed, and her voice was deeper than ever. "After all the only thing that counts really is spirit."

"Are you calling *me* vulgar, Frank?" asked Arrow with flashing eyes.

"No, of course she isn't," interrupted Beatrice.

"I wouldn't put it past you to go down in the kitchen when we're all in bed and have a good square meal on the sly."

Frank sprang to her feet.

"How dare you say that, Arrow! I'd never ask anybody to do what I'm not prepared to do myself. Have you known me all these years and do you think me capable of such a mean thing?"

"How is it you never take off any weight then?"

Frank gave a gasp and burst into a flood of tears.

"What a cruel thing to say! I've lost pounds and pounds."

She wept like a child. Her vast body shook, and great tears splashed on her mountainous bosom.

"Darling, I didn't mean it," cried Arrow.

She threw herself on her knees and enveloped what she could of Frank in her own plump arms. She wept, and the mascara ran down her cheeks.

"D'you mean to say I don't look thinner?" Frank sobbed. "After all I've gone through!"

"Yes, dear, of course you do," cried Arrow through her tears. "Everybody's noticed it."

Beatrice, though naturally of a placid disposition, began to cry gently. It was very pathetic. Indeed, it would have been a hard heart that failed to be moved by the sight of Frank, that lion-hearted woman, crying her eyes out. Presently, however, they dried their tears and had a little brandy and water, which every doctor had told them was the least fattening thing they could drink, and then they felt much better. They decided that Lena should have the nourishing food that had been ordered for her, and they made a solemn resolution not to let it disturb their equanimity. She was certainly a first-rate bridge player, and after all it was only for a fortnight. They would do whatever they could to make her stay enjoyable. They kissed one another warmly and separated for the night feeling strangely uplifted. Nothing should interfere with the wonderful friendship that had brought so much happiness into their three lives.

But human nature is weak. You must not ask too much of it. They ate grilled fish while Lena ate macaroni sizzling with cheese and butter; they ate grilled cutlets and boiled spinach while Lena ate *pâté de foie gras*; twice a week they ate hard-boiled eggs and raw tomatoes, while Lena ate peas swimming in cream and potatoes cooked in all sorts of delicious ways. The chef was a good chef, and he leapt at the opportunity afforded him to send up one dish more rich, tasty and succulent than the other.

"Poor Jim," sighed Lena, thinking of her husband, "he loved French cooking."

The butler disclosed the fact that he could make half a dozen kinds of cocktail, and Lena informed them that the doctor had recommended her to drink burgundy at luncheon and champagne at dinner. The three fat women persevered. They were gay, chatty and even hilarious (such is the natural gift that women have for deception), but Beatrice grew limp and forlorn, and Arrow's tender blue eyes acquired a steely glint. Frank's deep voice grew more raucous. It was when they played bridge that the strain showed itself. They had always been fond of talking over their hands, but their discussions had been friendly. Now a distinct bitterness crept in, and sometimes one pointed out a mistake to another with quite unnecessary frankness. Discussion turned to argument and argument to altercation. Sometimes the session ended in angry silence. Once Frank accused Arrow of deliberately letting her down. Two or three times Beatrice, the softest of the three, was reduced to tears. On another occasion Arrow flung down her cards and swept out of the room in a pet. Their tempers were getting frayed. Lena was the peacemaker.

"I think it's such a pity to quarrel over bridge," she said. "After all, it's only a game."

It was all very well for her. She had had a square meal and half a bottle of champagne. Besides, she had phenomenal luck. She was winning all their money. The score was put down in a book after each session, and hers mounted up day after day with unfailing regularity. Was there no justice in the world? They began to hate one another. And though they hated her too they could not resist confiding in her. Each of them went to her separately and told her how detestable the others were. Arrow said she was sure it was bad for her to see so much of women so much older than herself. She had a good mind to sacrifice her share of the lease and go to Venice for the rest of the summer. Frank told Lena that with her masculine mind it was too much to expect that she could be satisfied with anyone so frivolous as Arrow and so frankly stupid as Beatrice.

"I must have intellectual conversation," she boomed. "When you have a brain like mine you've got to consort with your intellectual equals."

Beatrice only wanted peace and quiet.

"Really I hate women," she said. "They're so unreliable; they're so malicious."

By the time Lena's fortnight drew to its close the three fat women were barely on speaking terms. They kept up appearances before Lena, but when she was not there made no pretences. They had got past quarrelling. They ignored each other with icy politeness.

Lena was going to stay with friends on the Italian Riviera, and Frank saw her off by the same train as that by which she had arrived. She was taking away with her a lot of their money.

"I don't know how to thank you," she said, as she got into the carriage. "I've had a wonderful visit."

If there was one thing that Frank Hickson prided herself on more than on being a match for any man it was that she was a gentlewoman, and her reply was perfect in its combination of majesty and graciousness.

"We've all enjoyed having you here, Lena," she said. "It's been a real treat."

But when she turned away from the departing train she heaved such a vast sigh of relief that the platform shook beneath her. She flung back her massive shoulders and strode home to the villa.

"Ouf!" she roared at intervals. "Ouf!"

She changed into her one-piece bathing suit, put on her espadrilles and a man's dressing gown (no nonsense about it) and went to Eden Roc. There was still time for a bathe before luncheon. She passed through the Monkey House, looking about her to say good morning to anyone she knew, for she felt on a sudden peace with mankind, and then stopped dead still. She could not believe her eyes. Beatrice was sitting at one of the tables, by herself; she wore the pyjamas she had bought at Molyneux's a day or two before, she had a string of pearls around her neck, and Frank's quick eyes saw that she had just had her hair waved; her cheeks, her eyes, her lips were made up. Fat, nay vast, as she was, none could deny that she was an extremely handsome woman. But what was she doing? With the slouching gait of the Neanderthal man which was Frank's characteristic walk she went up to Beatrice. In her black bathing dress Frank looked like the huge cetacean which the Japanese catch in the Torres Straits and which the vulgar call a sea cow.

"Beatrice, what are you doing?" she cried in her deep voice.

It was like the roll of thunder in the distant mountains. Beatrice looked at her coolly.

"Eating," she answered.

"Damn it, I can see you're eating."

In front of Beatrice was a plate of *croissants* and a plate of butter, a pot of strawberry jam, coffee and a jug of cream. Beatrice was spreading butter thick on the delicious hot bread, covering this with jam, and then pouring the thick cream over all.

"You'll kill yourself," said Frank.

"I don't care," mumbled Beatrice with her mouth full.

"You'll put on pounds and pounds."

"Go to hell!"

She actually laughed in Frank's face. My God, how good those *croissants* smelt!

"I'm disappointed in you, Beatrice. I thought you had more character."

"It's your fault. That blasted woman. You would have her down. For a fortnight I've watched her gorge like a hog. It's more than flesh and blood can stand. I'm going to have one square meal if I bust."

The tears welled up to Frank's eyes. Suddenly she felt very weak and womanly. She would have liked a strong man to take her on his knee and pet her and cuddle her and call her little baby names. Speechless, she sank down on a chair by Beatrice's side. A waiter came up. With a pathetic gesture she waved towards the coffee and *croissants*.

"I'll have the same," she sighed.

She listlessly reached out her hand to take a roll, but Beatrice snatched away the plate.

"No, you don't," she said. "You wait till you get your own."

Frank called her a name which ladies seldom apply to one another in affection. In a moment the waiter brought her *croissants*, butter, jam and coffee.

"Where's the cream, you fool?" she roared like a lioness at bay.

She began to eat. She ate gluttonously. The place was beginning to fill up with bathers coming to enjoy a cocktail or two after having done their duty by the sun and the sea. Presently Arrow strolled along with Prince Roccamare. She had on a beautiful silk wrap which she held tightly round her with one hand in order to look as slim as possible, and she bore her head high so that he should not see her double chin. She was laughing gaily. She felt like a girl. He had just told her (in Italian) that her eyes made the blue of the Mediterranean look like pea soup. He left her to go into the men's room to brush his sleek black hair, and they arranged to meet in five minutes for a drink. Arrow walked on to the women's room to put a little more rouge on her cheeks and a little more red on her lips. On her way she caught sight of Frank and Beatrice. She stopped. She could hardly believe her eyes.

"My God!" she cried. "You beasts. You hogs." She seized a chair. "Waiter."

Her appointment went clean out of her head. In the twinkling of an eye the waiter was at her side.

"Bring me what these ladies are having," she ordered.

Frank lifted her great heavy head from her plate.

"Bring me some *pâté de foie gras,*" she boomed.

"Frank!" cried Beatrice.

"Shut up."

"All right. I'll have some too."

The coffee was brought, and the hot rolls and cream and the *pâté de foie gras*, and they set to. They spread the cream on the *pâté* and they ate it. They devoured great spoonfuls of jam. They crunched the delicious crisp bread voluptuously. What was love to Arrow then? Let the Prince keep his palace in Rome and his castle in the Apennines. They did not speak. What they were about was much too serious. They ate with solemn, ecstatic fervour.

"I haven't eaten potatoes for twenty-five years," said Frank in a far-off brooding tone.

"Waiter," cried Beatrice, "bring fried potatoes for three."

"Très bien, madame."

The potatoes were brought. Not all the perfumes of Arabia smelt so sweet. They ate them with their fingers.

"Bring me a dry Martini," said Arrow.

"You can't have a dry Martini in the middle of a meal, Arrow," said Frank.

"Can't I? You wait and see."

"All right then. Bring me a double dry Martini," said Frank.

"Bring three double dry Martinis," said Beatrice.

They were brought and drunk at a gulp. The women looked at one another and sighed. The misunderstandings of the last fortnight dissolved, and the sincere affection each had for the other welled up again in their hearts. They could hardly believe that they had ever contemplated the possibility of severing a friendship that had brought them so much solid satisfaction. They finished the potatoes.

"I wonder if they've got any chocolate *éclairs*," said Beatrice.

"Of course they have."

And of course they had. Frank thrust one whole into her huge mouth, swallowed it and seized another, but before she ate it she looked at the other two and plunged a vindictive dagger into the heart of the monstrous Lena.

"You can say what you like, but the truth is she played a damned rotten game of bridge, really."

"Lousy," agreed Arrow.

But Beatrice suddenly thought she would like a meringue.

Contract

By Ring Lardner

WHEN the Sheltons were settled in their new home in the pretty little suburb of Linden, Mrs. Shelton was afraid nobody would call on them. Her husband was afraid somebody would. For ages Mrs. Shelton had bravely pretended to share her husband's aversion to a social life; he hated parties that numbered more than four people and she had convincingly, so she thought, played the role of indifference while declining invitations she would have given her right eye to accept. Shelton had not been fooled much, but his dislike of "crowds" was so great that he seldom sought to relieve her martyrdom by insisting that they "go" somewhere.

This was during the first six years of their connubial existence, while it was necessary to live, rather economically, in town. Recently, however, Shelton's magazine had advanced him to a position as associate editor and he was able, with the assistance of a benignant bond and mortgage company, to move into a house in Linden. Mrs. Shelton was sure suburbanites would be less tedious and unattractive than people they had known in the city and that it would not be fatal to her spouse to get acquainted and play around a little; anyway she could make friends with other wives, if they were willing, and perhaps enjoy afternoons of contract bridge, a game she had learned to love in three lessons. At the same time Shelton resolved to turn over a new leaf for his wife's sake and give her to understand that he was open for engagements, secretly hoping, as I have hinted, that Linden's denizens would treat them as if they were quarantined.

Mrs. Shelton's fears were banished, and Shelton's resolution put to a test, on an evening of their second week in the new house. They were dropped in on by Mr. and Mrs. Robert French who lived three blocks away. Mrs. French was pretty and Shelton felt inclined to like her until she remarked how fascinating it must be to edit a magazine and meet Michael Arlen. French had little to say, being occupied most of the while in a petting party with his mustache.

Mrs. Shelton showed Mrs. French her seven hooked rugs. Mrs. French said, "Perfectly darling!" seven times, inquired where each of the seven had been procured and did not listen to the answers. Shelton served highballs of eighty dollar Scotch he had bought from a Linden bootlegger. French commented favorably on the Scotch. Shelton thought it was terrible himself and that French was a poor judge, or was being polite, or was deceived by some flavor lurking in the mustache. Mrs. Shelton ran out of hooked rugs and Mrs. French asked whether they played contract. Mrs. Shelton hesitated from habit. Shelton swallowed hard and replied that they did, and liked it very much.

"That's wonderful!" said Mrs. French. "Because the Wilsons have moved to Chicago. They were crazy about contract and we used to have a party every Wednesday night; two tables—the Wilsons, ourselves, and the Dittmars and Camerons. It would be just grand if you two would take the Wilsons' place. We have dinner at somebody's house and next Wednesday is our turn. Could you come?"

Mrs. Shelton again hesitated and Shelton (to quote O. O. McIntyre) once more took the bull by the horns.

"It sounds fine!" he said. "We haven't anything else on for that night, have we, dear?"

His wife uttered an astonished no and the Frenches left.

"What in the world has happened to you?" demanded Mrs. Shelton.

"Nothing at all. They seem like nice people and we've got to make friends here. Besides, it won't be bad playing cards."

"I don't know about contract," said Mrs. Shelton doubtfully. "You've got good card sense, and the only time you played it, you were all right. But I'm afraid I'll make hideous mistakes."

"Why should you? And even if you do, what of it?"

"These people are probably whizzes."

"I don't care if they're Lenz's mother-in-law."

"But you'll care if they criticize you."

"Of course I will. People, and especially strangers, have no more right to criticize your bridge playing than your clothes or your complexion."

"You know that's silly. Bridge is a game."

"Tennis is a game, too. But how often do you hear one tennis player say to another, 'You played that like an old fool!'?"

"You're not partners in tennis."

"You are in doubles. However, criticism in bridge is not confined to partners. I've made bonehead plays in bridge (I'll admit it), and been laughed at and scolded for them by opponents who ought to have kissed me. It's a conviction of most bridge players, and some golf players, that God sent them into the world to teach. At that, what they tell you isn't intended for your edification and future good. It's just a way of announcing 'I'm smart and you're a lunkhead.' And to my mind it's a revelation of bad manners and bad sportsmanship. If I ask somebody what I did wrong, that's different. But when they volunteer—"

It was an old argument and Mrs. Shelton did not care to continue it. She knew she couldn't win and she was sleepy. Moreover, she was so glad they were "going out" on her husband's own insistence that she felt quite kindly toward him. She did hope, though, that their new acquaintances would suppress their educational complex if any.

On Wednesday night this hope was knocked for a double row of early June peas. Mrs. Shelton was elected to play with French, Mrs. Cameron and Mr. Dittmar. Mrs. Cameron was what is referred to as a statuesque blonde, but until you were used to her you could think of nothing but her nostrils, where she might easily have carried two after-dinner mints. Mr. Dittmar appeared to be continuing to enjoy his meal long after it was over. And French had to deal one-handed to be sure his mustache remained loyal. These details distracted Mrs. Shelton's mind to such an extent that she made a few errors and was called for them. But she didn't mind that and her greatest distraction was caused by words and phrases that came from the other table, where her husband was engaged with Mr. Cameron, Mrs. Dittmar and the hostess.

The French cocktails had been poured from an eyedropper and Shelton maintained perfect control of his temper and tongue. His polite reception of each criticism was taken as a confession of ignorance and a willingness to learn, and his three tablemates were quick to assume the role of faculty, with him as the entire student-body. He was stepped on even when he was dummy, his partner at the time, Mrs. Dittmar, attributing the loss of a trick to the manner in which he had laid out his cards, the light striking the nine of diamonds in such a way as to make her think it was an honor.

Mrs. Dittmar had married a man much younger than herself and was trying to disguise that fact by acting much younger than he. An eight-year-old child who is kind of backward hardly ever plays contract bridge; otherwise, if you didn't look at Mrs. Dittmar and judged only by her antics and manner of speech, you would have thought Dittmar had spent the final hours of his courtship waiting outside the sub-primary to take her home. Mrs. French, when she was picking flaws in Shelton's play, sought to make him feel at home by asking intelligent questions about his work—"Do the people who draw the illustrations read the stories first?" "Does H. C. Witwer talk Negro dialect all the time?" And "How old is Peter B. Kinney?" Cameron, from whom Work, Lenz, Whitehead and Shepard had plagiarized the game, was frankly uninterested in anything not connected with it. The stake was half a cent a point and the pains he took to see that his side's score was correct or better proved all the rumors about the two Scotchmen.

Mrs. Shelton was well aware that her husband was the politest man in the world when sober; yet he truly amazed her that evening by his smiling acquiescence to all that was said. From the snatches she overheard, she knew he must be afire inside and it was really wonderful of him not to show it.

There was a time when Mrs. Dittmar passed and he passed and Cameron bid two spades. Mrs. French passed and Mrs. Dittmar bid three hearts, a denial of her partner's spades if Shelton ever heard one. Shelton passed and Cameron went three hearts, which stood. Shelton held four spades to the nine, four diamonds to the king, two small hearts and the eight, six, and five of clubs. He led the trey of diamonds. I am not broadcasting the battle play by play, but when it was over, "Oh, partner! Any other opening and we could have set them," said Mrs. French.

"My! My! My! My! Leading away from a king!" gurgled the child-wife.

"That lead was all that saved us," said Cameron.

They waited for Shelton to apologize and explain, all prepared to scrunch him if he did either.

"I guess I made a mistake," he said.

"Haven't you played much bridge?" asked Mrs. French.

"Evidently not enough," he replied.

"It's a game you can't learn in a minute," said Cameron.

"Never you mind!" said Mrs. Dittmar. "I've played contract ever since it came out, and Daddy still scolds me terribly for some of the things I do."

Shelton presumed that Daddy was her husband. Her father must be dead or at least too feeble to scold.

There was a time when a hand was passed around.

"Oh! A goulash!" crowed Mrs. Dittmar.

"Do you play them, Mr. Shelton?" asked his hostess.

"Yes," said Shelton.

"Mrs. Shelton," called Mrs. Dittmar to the other table, "does your big man play goulashes?"

"Oh, yes," said Mrs. Shelton.

"You're sure you know what they are," said Cameron to Shelton.

"I've played them often," said the latter.

"A goulash," said the hostess, "is where the hand is passed and then we all put our hands together like this and cut them and the dealer deals five around twice and then three. It makes crazy hands, but it's thrilling."

"And the bidding is different," said Mrs. Dittmar, his partner at this stage. "Big mans mustn't get too wild."

Shelton, who had dealt, looked at his hand, and saw no temptation to get wild; at least, not any wilder than he was. He had the king, queen and jack of spades, four silly hearts, four very young clubs and two diamonds of no standing. He passed. Cameron bid three clubs and Mrs. Dittmar four diamonds. That was enough to make game (they already had thirty), and when Mrs. French went by, Shelton unhesitatingly did the same. So did Cameron. It developed that Mrs. Dittmar had the ace, king, jack, ten and another diamond. Cameron had none and Mrs. French reeked with them. The bidder was set two. Her honors counted one hundred and the opponents' net profit was two hundred, Mrs. Dittmar being vulnerable, or "venerable" as Mrs. French laughingly, but not very tactfully, called it.

Cameron lighted into Mrs. French for not doubling Mrs. Dittmar and Mrs. French observed that she guessed she knew what she was doing. Shelton hoped this would develop into a brawl, but it was forgotten when Mrs. Dittmar asked him querulously why he had not shown her his spades, a suit of which she had held the ace, ten to five.

"We're lucky, partner," said Mrs. French to Cameron. "They could have made four spades like a breeze."

"I'd have lost only the ace of hearts and queen of diamonds," said Mrs. Dittmar, doubtless figuring that the maid would have disposed of her two losing clubs when she swept next morning.

"In this game, everything depends on the bidding,"

said Mrs. French to Shelton. "You *must* give your partner all the information you can."

"Don't coach him!" said Cameron with an exasperating laugh. "He's treating us pretty good."

"Maybe," said Mrs. French to Mrs. Dittmar, "he would have shown you his spades if you had bid three diamonds instead of four."

"But you see," said Mrs. Dittmar, "we needed four for game and I didn't know if he'd think of that."

And there was a time when Shelton bid a fair no trump and was raised to three by his partner, Cameron, who held king, queen, ten to five hearts and the ace of clubs for a re-entry. The outstanding hearts were bunched in Mrs. French's hand, Shelton himself having the lone ace. After he had taken a spade trick, led his ace of hearts and then a low club to make all of dummy's hearts good (which turned out to be impossible), he put over two deep sea finesses of the eight and nine of diamonds from the dummy hand, made four odd and heard Cameron murmur, "A fool for luck!"

"My! What a waste of good hearts!" said Mrs. Dittmar, ignoring the facts that they weren't good hearts, that if he had continued with them, Mrs. French would have taken the jack and led to her (Mrs. Dittmar's) four good spade tricks, and that with the ace of clubs gone, Shelton couldn't have got back in the dummy's hands with a pass from Judge Landis.

At the close of a perfect evening, the Sheltons were six dollars ahead and invited to the Dittmars' the following Wednesday. Mrs. Shelton expected an explosion on the way home, but was agreeably disappointed. Shelton seemed quite cheerful. He had a few jocose remarks to make about their new pals, but gave the impression that he had enjoyed himself. Knowing him as she did, she might have suspected that a plot was hatching in his mind. However, his behavior was disarming and she thought he had at last found a "crowd" he didn't object to, that they would now be neighborly and gregarious for the first time in their married life.

On the train from the city Friday afternoon, Shelton encountered Gale Bartlett, the writer, just returned from abroad. Bartlett was one of the star contributors to Shelton's magazine and it was he who had first suggested Linden when Shelton was considering a suburban home. He had a place there himself though most of his time was spent in Paris and he was back now for only a brief stay.

"How do you like it?" he asked.

"Fine," said Shelton.

"Whom have you met?"

"Three married couples, the Camerons, the Frenches and the Dittmars."

"Good Lord!" said Bartlett. "I don't know the Dittmars but otherwise you're slumming. Cameron and French are new rich who probably made their money in a hotel washroom. I think they met their wives on an excursion to Far Rockaway. How did you happen to get acquainted?"

"The Frenches called on us, and Wednesday night we went to their house for dinner and bridge."

"Bridge!"

"Contract bridge at that."

"Well, maybe Dittmar's a contractor. But from what I've seen of the Frenches and Camerons, they couldn't even cut the cards without smearing them with shoe polish. You break loose from them before they forget themselves and hand you a towel."

"We're going to the Dittmars' next Wednesday night."

"Either call it off or keep it under your hat. I'll introduce you to people that are people! I happen to know them because my wife went to their sisters' boarding school. I'll see that you get the entrée and then you can play bridge with bridge players."

Shelton brightened at the prospect. He knew his wife was too kind-hearted to wound the Camerons *et al* by quitting them cold and it was part of his scheme, all of it in fact, to make them do the quitting. With the conviction that she would be more than compensated by the promised acquaintance of people they both could really like, he lost what few scruples he had against separating her from people who sooner or later would drive him to the electric chair. The thing must be done at the first opportunity, next Wednesday at the Dittmars'. It would be kind of fun, but unpleasant, too, the unpleasant part consisting in the mental anguish it would cause her and the subsequent days, not many he hoped, when she wouldn't be speaking to him at all.

Fate, in the form of one of Mrs. Shelton's two-day headaches, brought about the elimination of the unpleasant part. The ache began Wednesday afternoon and from past experience, she knew she would not be able to sit through a dinner or play cards that night. She telephoned her husband.

"Say we can't come," was his advice.

"But I hate to do that. They'll think we don't want to and they won't ask us again. I wish you'd go, and maybe they could ask somebody in to take my place, I don't suppose you'd consider that, would you?"

Shelton thought it over a moment and said yes, he would.

Before retiring to her darkened room and her bed, Mrs. Shelton called up Mrs. Dittmar. Mrs. Dittmar expressed her sympathy in baby talk and said it was all right for Mr. Shelton to come alone; it was more than all right, Mrs. Shelton gathered, because Mrs. Dittmar's brother was visiting her and they would be just eight.

Shelton, who had learned long ago that his wife did not want him around when her head was threatening to burst open, stayed in town until six o'clock, preparing himself for the evening's task with liberal doses of the business manager's week-old rye. He was not going to be tortured by any drought such as he had endured at the Frenches'. He arrived at the party in grand shape and, to his surprise, was plied with cocktails potent enough to keep him on edge.

Mrs. Dittmar's brother (she called him her dreat, big b'udder) was an amateur jazz pianist. Or rather, peeanist. He was proving his amateur standing when Shelton got there and something in the way he treated "Rhapsody in Blue" made Shelton resolve to open fire at once. His eagerness was increased when, on the way to the dining room, Mrs. Dittmar observed that her b'udder had not played much contract "either" and she must be sure and not put them (Shelton and B'udder) at the same table, for they might draw each other as partners and that would hardly be fair.

Dinner began and so did Shelton.

"A week ago," he said, "you folks criticised my bridge playing."

The Camerons, Dittmars and Frenches looked queer.

"You didn't mind it, I hope," said Mrs. Dittmar. "We were just trying to teach you."

"I didn't mind it much," said Shelton. "But I was just wondering whether it was good manners for one person to point out another person's mistakes when the other person didn't ask to have them pointed out."

"Why," said Cameron, "when one person don't know as much about a thing as other people, it's their duty to correct him."

"You mean just in bridge," said Shelton.

"I mean in everything," said Cameron.

"And the person criticised or corrected has no right to resent it?" said Shelton.

"Certainly not!"

"Does everybody here agree with that?"

"Yes," "Of course," "Sure," came from the others.

"Well, then," said Shelton, "I think it's my duty to tell you, Mr. Cameron, that soup should be dipped away from you and not toward you."

There was a puzzled silence, then a laugh, to which Cameron contributed feebly.

"If that's right I'm glad to know it, and I certainly don't resent your telling me," he said.

"It looks like Mr. Shelton was out for revenge," said Mrs. Cameron.

"And I must inform you, Mrs. Cameron," said Shelton, "that 'like' is not a conjunction. 'It looks as if Mr. Shelton were out for revenge' would be the correct phrasing."

A smothered laugh at the expense of Mrs. Cameron, whose embarrassment showed itself in a terrifying distension of the nostrils. Shelton decided not to pick on her again.

"Let's change the subject," said Mrs. Dittmar. "Mr. Shelton's a mean, bad man and he'll make us cwy."

"That verb," said Shelton, "is cry, not cwy. It is spelled c–r–y."

"Tell a story, Bob," said Mrs. French to her husband.

"Well, let's see," said French. "I'll tell the one about the Scotchman and the Jew playing golf. Stop me if anybody's heard it."

"I have, for one," said Shelton.

"Maybe the others haven't," said French.

"They must have been unconscious for years," said Shelton. "But go ahead and tell it. I knew I couldn't stop you."

French went ahead and told it, and the others laughed as a rebuke to Shelton.

Cameron wanted things understood.

"You see," he said, "the reason we made a few little criticisms of your bridge game was because we judged you were a new beginner."

"I think 'beginner' is enough, without the 'new,' " said Shelton. "I don't know any old beginners excepting, perhaps, people old in years who are doing something or taking up something for the first time. But probably you judged I was a beginner at bridge because of mistakes I made, and you considered my apparent inexperience justified you in criticising me."

"Yes," said Cameron.

"Well," said Shelton, "I judge from observing Mrs. French eat her fish that she is a new beginner at eating and I take the liberty of stating that the fork ought never to be conveyed to the mouth with the left hand, even by a left-handed eater. To be sure, these forks are salad forks, not fish forks, as Mrs. Dittmar may believe. But even salad forks, substituting for fish forks, must not be carried mouthward by the left hand."

A storm was gathering and Mrs. Cameron sought to ward it off. She asked Mrs. Dittmar what had become of Peterson, a butler.

"He just up and left me last week," said Mrs. Dittmar. "He was getting too impudent, though, and you can bet I didn't object to him going."

" '*His* going'," said Shelton. "A participle used as a substantive is modified in the possessive."

Everyone pretended not to hear him.

"This new one is grand!" said Mrs. Dittmar. "I didn't get up till nearly eleven o'clock this morning—"

"Eleven!" exclaimed Mrs. French.

"Yes. Imagine!" said Mrs. Dittmar. "The itta girl just overslept herself, that's all."

"Mrs. Dittmar," said Shelton, "I have no idea who the itta girl is, but I am interested in your statement that she overslept herself. Would it be possible for her, or any other itta girl, to oversleep somebody else? If it were a sleeping contest, I should think 'outsleep' would be preferable, but even so I can't understand how a girl of any size outsleeps herself."

The storm broke. Dittmar sprang to his feet.

"That's enough, Shelton!" he bellowed. "We've had enough of this nonsense! More than enough!"

"I think," said Shelton, "that the use of the word 'enough' three times in one short speech is more than enough. It grates on me to hear or read a word reiterated like that. I suggest as synonyms 'plenty,' 'a sufficiency,' 'an abundance,' 'a plethora.' "

"Shut your smart aleck mouth and get out!"

"Carl! Carl! Mustn't lose temper!" said Mrs. Dittmar. "Lose temper and can't digest food. Daddy mustn't lose temper and be sick all nighty night."

"Shelton just thinks he's funny," said Cameron.

"He's drunk and he'll leave my house at once!" said Dittmar.

"If that's the way you feel about it," said Shelton.

He stopped on the way out to bid Mrs. Dittmar's brother good-night.

"Good-night, B'udder old boy," he said. "I'm glad to have met you, but sorry to learn you're deaf."

"Deaf! What makes you think I'm deaf?"

"I understood your sister to say you played the piano by ear."

Knowing his wife would have taken something to

make her sleep, and therefore not afraid of disturbing her, Shelton went home, got out a bottle of Linden Scotch and put the finishing touches on his bender. In the morning Mrs. Shelton was a little better and came to the breakfast table where he was fighting an egg.

"Well, what kind of time did you have?"

"Glorious! Much more exciting than at the Frenches'. Mrs. Dittmar's brother is a piano playing fool."

"Oh, wasn't there any bridge then?"

"No. Just music and banter."

"Maybe the brother can't play contract and I spoiled the party by not going."

"Oh, no. *You* didn't spoil the party!"

"And do we go to the Camerons' next Wednesday?"

"I don't believe so. Nothing was said."

They did go next Wednesday night to the palatial home of E. M. Pardee, a friend of Gale Bartlett's and one of the real aristocrats of Linden. After dinner, Mrs. Pardee asked the Sheltons whether they played contract, and they said they did. The Pardees, not wishing to impoverish the young immigrants, refused to play "families." They insisted on cutting and Shelton cut Mrs. Pardee.

"Oh, Mr. Shevlin," she said at the end of the first hand, "why *didn't* you lead me a club? You *must* watch the discards!"

Author's Postscript: This story won't get me anything but the money I am paid for it. Even if it be read by those with whom I usually play—Mr. C., Mrs. W., Mr. T., Mrs. R. and the rest—they will think I mean two other fellows and tear into me like wolves next time I bid a slam and make one odd.

Last Board

By Ron Klinger

THE Bridgerama commentator's voice boomed across the audience. *Bermuda Bowl as good as over . . . three boards left . . . Challengers 33 imps down . . . even the Old Master's magic can't help now . . .*

The Old Master looked down at his cards, though their pasteboard patterns were indelibly etched in his mind. Three boards. He glanced across at his partner. Zettner's brow was furrowed too. Despite some good pickups in this last session, they must still be at least 30 or more imps down. The champions, Frawley-Kinston, were silent—they knew the title was once again theirs.

Five years they had held the world crown, and the sixth was merely minutes away. Fifty-six imps up—16 boards to play. No team in the Bowl could recover that ground. Even counting some sure losses, they had to be well ahead.

As the Old Master waited for the next hand, the old question rose once more. Could this be the one, the perfect hand, the work of art? What was the perfect hand?

Was Culbertson right? Was it nothing more than success stemming from opponents' errors? What was beauty in bridge anyway? Was it nine top tricks in three notrump? Though he couldn't pin it down, he felt that there had to be something more, some intangible combination of power in the cards.

Suddenly, he felt very tired, recalling the dilemma in which he constantly found himself in his 40 years' playing. Percentages or elegance? Play to win or play for perfection? Before him rose the shades of games and tournaments lost because he could never quite resolve which he wanted. He remembered the hand that had cost him the Olympiad because he played for the squeeze rather than the finesse.

Frawley's pass woke him from his reverie. The dream of the perfect hand faded. His partner opened one diamond and Kinston interposed two hearts, a weak bid based on long hearts. The Old Master looked at his hand:

♠ J 7 6 4 ♡ — ◊ 9 ♣ A K Q J 9 7 6 4

A straightforward three clubs? Four clubs to emphasize their solidity? The scientists would know—they would get to the cold grand slam or avoid the unmakable small slam, but their tortuous approach repelled him—too often it pointed the way to astute defenders. Neither side was vulnerable.

"Six clubs."

He smiled wryly, imagining what the commentators would be saying. A leap into the unknown. It could be disastrous, but it was no time to be dainty: The likely heart lead might give him time to work on the diamonds.

Frawley looked up quickly, paused slightly, and passed. Zettner passed and Kinston doubled. Lightner.

A diamond lead. A bad sign. All passed, and the two of diamonds was led.

NORTH
♠ A K 3
♡ K J 8 5
♢ Q 10 8 7 5
♣ 8

WEST
♠ Q 9 2
♡ A 6 2
♢ J 4 3 2
♣ 10 5 3

EAST
♠ 10 8 5
♡ Q 10 9 7 4 3
♢ A K 6
♣ 2

SOUTH
♠ J 7 6 4
♡ —
♢ 9
♣ A K Q J 9 7 6 4

The Old Master called for a low diamond and the king of diamonds won.

In the Closed Room, North-South reached three no trump and made 10 tricks, the commentator told the audience. *If six clubs is made, the challengers will gain 12 imps, but unless East makes the fatal ace of diamonds continuation, South will have to lose a spade ultimately. I predict East will exit with the two of clubs.*

East thought for some time, then the trump appeared. The Old Master won and drew two more rounds of trumps, discarding two hearts from dummy. East discarded the seven-four of hearts. The Old Master stopped to think. East began with the ace-king of diamonds. Not the ace of hearts—that would be too strong for a weak jump-interpose. Six hearts headed by the queen. Kinston was strict about suit quality. With seven he would have bid three hearts, without the queen the suit would have been too poor. Probably he was 3-6-3-1 with 9 points. That must be all, for the queen of spades would also make the hand too strong for a "weak" two hearts. So, West held the queen of spades, ace of hearts and the jack of diamonds. That might be just too much to manage.

Suddenly, the Old Master was no longer tired. As he pieced the play together, conviction refreshed him. He played three more rounds of clubs, pitching a spade, a diamond, and the jack of hearts. West threw a diamond and two hearts; East discarded hearts. This was the position:

	NORTH	
	♠ A K	
	♡ K	
	◇ Q 10 8	
	♣ —	
WEST		EAST
♠ Q 9 2		♠ 10 8 5
♡ A		♡ Q
◇ J 4		◇ A 6
♣ —		♣ —
	SOUTH	
	♠ J 7 6 4	
	♡ —	
	◇ —	
	♣ 6 4	

The Old Master played another club and watched West writhe. If West discarded a spade the ace-king would drop the queen, while a diamond discard would allow the jack to be pinned. West studied for a long time and finally ditched the ace of hearts. But the hand was an open book. A spade to dummy, and the king of hearts put West in the vice again. He threw the four of diamonds; the Old Master reached across and touched the queen of diamonds, murmuring softly, "The pin is mightier than the sword." As East covered and West dropped the jack, the hand was over.

A triple squeeze . . . brilliancy . . . Old Master still has spark of genius . . . 10 years since he played internationally . . . included in Challengers team as sentimental gesture . . . long career . . . now proved back at best . . . assured of second in world . . . 12 imps to Challengers . . . not enough to stave off defeat . . .

In the Open Room, Frawley growled bitterly at Kinston.

"A spade return at trick two beats it. Takes out his entry prematurely."

"Sure. And I also knew South didn't have jack-nine-fourth in spades, didn't I?"

The Old Master looked at them sorrowfully. Why was there always so much rancor at the top? He looked as Frawley sat, tight-lipped, stubborn—Frawley, contemptuous of opponents and partners alike—acknowledged as the world's best, yet unable to brook losing a game or a match.

These thoughts were brushed aside as the Old Master picked up the cards. Second-last hand. At least they had made a fight of it. They were vulnerable against not. His partner, dealer, passed. So did Kinston. He looked at

♠ A ♡ A K 6 2 ◇ K J 10 9 2 ♣ K 4 3

and opened one diamond.

Frawley cleared his throat. "Three spades."

Pass from Zettner, pass from Kinston, what now? Four hearts."

"Four spades."

The Old Master looked at Frawley curiously. A bead of perspiration rested on Frawley's brow. Was he shaken, that fine bridge mind, the leading theorist in the world? Frawley, who had expounded, "preempt what you are worth," breaking his own tenets? Three spades, then four spades. Why not four spades at once? The Old Master noticed a slight tremble in Frawley's left hand.

Zettner, patting his hair nervously, tugging at a loose strand, pondered, then bid five hearts. Kinston's double was loud and crisp, and everyone passed. Frawley pulled out the king of spades, and dummy came down.

NORTH
♠ 6 3
♡ J 8 5 4
♢ A Q 7
♣ J 10 9 2

WEST
♠ K Q J 10 8 7 5 2
♡ 7
♢ 8 6
♣ 8 5

EAST
♠ 9 4
♡ Q 10 9 3
♢ 5 4 3
♣ A Q 7 6

SOUTH
♠ A
♡ A K 6 2
♢ K J 10 9 2
♣ K 4 3

Closed Room . . . four spades doubled . . . two down . . . plus 300 to Champions . . . headed for big swing . . . South must lose two hearts and a club at least . . . five diamonds a chance . . . five hearts hopeless . . . bad split . . .

The Old Master surveyed the two hands. East would obviously have four trumps at least, maybe five. Prospects were not good. Winning the ace of spades, he played the jack of diamonds. Frawley played the eight of diamonds as a matter of doubleton reflex, then pulled his hand away as if burnt. The Old Master suddenly saw a glimmer of hope as dummy's seven of diamonds became a third entry. Could West have a key singleton in trumps?

Dummy's ace of diamonds won, and the jack of hearts was played. The Old Master felt his heart pounding . . . was there a chance after all? If East held Q-10-9-7 of hearts, all was lost. The queen topped the jack, the Old Master played his ace and looked at Frawley's card. The seven of hearts.

The first hurdle was over. Would the other cards behave also? The Old Master moved into the strange world of bridge intuition. Lines of play ran through his mind, the cards swirled into patterns, disappeared, regrouped, blended into a position six tricks away. The Old Master, satisfied with his plan, played the ten of diamonds to the queen and called for dummy's jack of clubs. Kinston played low. So did the others. Another club from dummy. This time Kinston took his ace and forced South with a spade return. The Old Master ruffed with the two of hearts and reviewed the situation.

NORTH
♠ —
♡ 8 5 4
◇ 7
♣ J 2

WEST		EAST
♠ Q J 10 8 7 5		♠ —
♡ —		♡ 10 9 3
◇ —		◇ 5
♣ —		♣ Q 7

SOUTH
♠ —
♡ K 6
◇ K 9 2
♣ K

No, there was no flaw. It had to be right. He played the king of clubs and crossed to dummy's seven of diamonds with his well-preserved deuce. The Old Master carefully picked over the end position he had seen before. There was no escape.

A small trump was played from dummy. East sat there thinking. He would have to split the ten-nine, thought the Old Master; if not, I win with the six of hearts, cash the king of hearts, and play a diamond, discarding my losing club from dummy.

Kinston thought interminably; finally, the nine of hearts. Declarer played the king of hearts, and then, luxuriously, treasuring the touch, the Old Master played a diamond and put the eight of hearts on from dummy.

Brilliant timing and end-play, the 'Rama commentator shrieked shrilly. *If East overruffs and plays a club, South ruffs in hand and ruffs the last diamond in dummy. If East overruffs and plays a trump, South wins and his hand is high. And if East discards his club, dummy's club promotes South's six of trumps en passant . . .*

In the Open Room, the Old Master wondered what was happening. Had the commentators seen the position as he had? Was there any chance of snatching victory from the jaws of defeat? The last two hands had to be gains, but how close was the fight? He could not hear the commentator.

. . . Plus 850 to Challengers . . . 11 imps . . . exciting finish . . . Champions still 10 imps up . . . additional drama . . . youth versus age . . . fantastic finale . . .

The audience hushed as the lights on the Bridgerama board flickered, then lit up the last hand.

NORTH
♠ A Q 7
♡ A K 10 6
◇ 8 6
♣ A K J 4

WEST
♠ 10 8 5 4
♡ J 7 5 3
◇ 7
♣ 10 9 7 2

EAST
♠ K 9
♡ 9 8 2
◇ K 9 4 2
♣ Q 6 5 3

SOUTH
♠ J 6 3 2
♡ Q 4
◇ A Q J 10 5 3
♣ 8

The commentator broke into an excited jabber. *Closed Room . . . Champions overboard . . . reached seven notrump . . . trying to duplicate probable gamble in Open Room . . . two down . . . Challengers have chance . . . must stay out of slam . . . game gives them 11 imps and victory . . . slam doomed . . . bad diamond break . . . spade finesse loses . . .*

In the Open Room, the silence was almost unbearable. The Old Master knew what the others were thinking. Last board. How small was the margin? Was there a chance or was the match already over? The audience already knew, but the players had to gauge the results for themselves. He looked at this hand. Six diamonds and four spades. The opposition was vulnerable, they were not. He was second to speak. The age-old question arose, to preempt or not to preempt? The "authorities" all said not to preempt with a side four-card major, also that a second-hand preempt was less desirable since one opponent had already passed. He made up his mind. The thought of the perfect hand casually flitted across his mind. He dismissed it as Kinston passed quickly.

"Three diamonds."

Pass from Frawley, nervously. Zettner sat for an eternity. The Old Master knew he must be thinking about slam chances, and was pleased his diamond suit was respectable. Preempts at favorable vulnerability can often be filthy.

As the minutes toiled on, the audience became restless. *Three notrump . . . why doesn't he bid three notrump? . . . how can he think of a slam with nothing in diamonds? . . . five diamonds is all right too . . .*

"Six diamonds."

The audience groaned.

Three passes followed quickly. Frawley sat for some time considering his lead, then the ten of clubs hit the table. The Old Master surveyed the dummy and his own hand.

The slam was reasonable. Had they reached it in the other room? If he didn't lose a diamond trick, the slam was home. With a diamond loser, he still had chances—the jack of hearts might fall in three rounds, the spade finesse was there, and the queen of clubs might appear. He looked at the lead. The ten of clubs. Had Frawley led away from the queen? Would the club finesse work at trick one? Not a tempting lead against a small slam. The Old Master played the king of clubs and took the diamond finesse. The queen of diamonds held. He played the four of hearts to the king and played another diamond to the jack. Frawley showed out.

If he makes the slam, Challengers win by 4 imps . . . if he goes down, Champions have lucky escape . . .

The Old Master searched his mind. It was merely a matter of taking all the chances in the right order. One of them would probably succeed. But the quest for perfection tortured him. Painfully, he scanned dummy again. Once more he searched the position, wondering why he was hesitating, why he did not continue.

Suddenly he saw it, and everything else faded except the patterns of force generated by the cards as they glided into their predestined place. Again the testing of each play, racked by the error of his original analysis, soothed by what he could see unfolding before him. Finally, he played the ace of diamonds, discarding dummy's low spade. Then the queen of hearts, dropping dummy's six on it.

NORTH
♠ A Q
♡ A 10
◇ —
♣ A J 4

SOUTH
♠ J 6 3 2
♡ —
◇ 10 5 3
♣ —

The Old Master considered the final position cherishingly. The aces . . . the master cards . . . one in each suit in dummy . . . each supported by a different lower honor, side by side . . . each tenace agape waiting for East to yield up the twelfth trick . . . each suit having a finesse available in it . . . but the only finesse taken successfully turning out not to gain a trick . . . the suits blending together, in harmony and unison, to succeed no matter where the enemy cards lay.

The victory was his. He had but to take it. With trembling fingers he took the ten of diamonds, putting East on lead, softly asked for dummy's four of clubs, and whispered gently to the opposition a single word.

"Checkmate."

Character

By Stephen White

(With a modest bow to P. G. W.)

"I NEVER would have believed it of him," said the Underbidder, looking up from his newspaper. "Though of course I scarcely knew him."

"I knew him better than you did," said the Doubler, "and I would have laughed if someone had suggested it."

"But here it is," said the Underbidder. "Two years for larceny and fraud. He admitted he was guilty."

"He always seemed like a perfect gentleman," sighed the Doubler. "I simply never would have believed it."

"And I," broke in the Old Kibitzer, "I suspected it all along."

Both men turned to him incredulously. "You knew it?" said the Underbidder. "You never mentioned it. You never said a word about it."

"Of course not," said the Old Kibitzer. "You probably would have laughed at me. Nevertheless, I repeat that I suspected it."

"How?" asked the Doubler. "What could have made you suspect him?"

"I saw him," said the Old Kibitzer awesomely. "I saw him pass a two-bid."

The two men looked at the Old Kibitzer in unbelief; then began to laugh. "Do you mean to sit there and tell us," said the Doubler, "that you would infer a criminal mind from a man's actions at a bridge table?"

"Certainly," he was told. "A man who will pass a two-bid is capable of almost anything. He shows the temper of his mind with every move he makes at the table."

"You are talking nonsense," said the Underbidder. "Bridge is a game, you know."

"Certainly it is. At the same time it is a model of life itself. You two have just cut out of a rubber?" They nodded. "I see," said the Old Kibitzer, "that a few of our better flag-flyers are at the table. You will have quite a wait until you can cut in again, and I will be pleased to tell you a little story while you are sitting out. You will find it has a definite bearing on the subject."

I don't believe (began the Old Kibitzer) that either of you belonged to the Club when Harold Phillips joined it. It was several years ago, when we had quarters across the hall. He was in Law School at the time, and was forced to stay here in the city during one summer in connection with his studies, and with a good deal of his time unoccupied he took to dropping in at the Club now and then for a rubber or two.

He was well liked immediately. Of course, just out of college as he was, he had a tendency to radical ideas. He had moved with a free-thinking crowd at school, read the wrong books, and shared youth's love for the sensational: as a result he frequently bid three card majors and underled aces. However, as he became more acquainted with our little group he settled down considerably and by the end of the month he was being treated as one of the regulars. Everyone admitted that he was a personable young man, always with a quip on his lips, and a brilliant bridge player.

Having joined the club in the summer, he was necessarily unacquainted with that large group of our members which leaves the city each year with the onset of hot weather and shows up again only when fall is upon us. Hence it was some months before he met Lucy Martin. This, of course, means nothing to either of you two gentlemen, since Lucy Martin was also before your time here. Let me say, however, that she was one of the brightest spots this club has ever possessed. She had, at that time, already won the Lady's Pairs twice, and finished well up in the lists regularly at the Wednesday afternoon duplicates. Her handling of dummy reversal hands was a delight to behold, and her cross-ruff technique was crisp and decisive. I have heard it said she was beautiful as well; it was probably true.

It happened that I was present when Harold and Lucy met. The club champion had been forced to break a date with Harold for our Monday night duplicate, and Harold had asked me to play with him. Needless to say I was pleased at the opportunity, and we were at Table 1, North and South, doing quite well, when Lucy, playing with old Mrs. Harris, came to our table. Naturally, when the two women sat down I began at once to count my cards—as required in the rules—and as a result I failed to notice that Harold had become strangely flustered and had turned a deep shade of unbecoming red. Mrs. Harris told me of that later: She said also that his Adam's apple was quivering spasmodically and he was evincing a disposition to choke. In view of what happened immediately after, I can well believe it.

Harold was dealer on the first hand and passed. I opened the bidding light in third position, and was startled and shocked to hear Harold respond with three notrump.

Need I say we were beaten two tricks, vulnerable? At the conclusion of play, I reached over to verify Harold's holding, and discovered he held a weak two honor-trick hand. Naturally, I began to remonstrate with him, but he seemed to be paying me no attention. His eyes were riveted on Lucy.

I scarcely should be forced to go into more details: You must realize by now that I had been victimized by love at first sight. Harold had become enamored of the girl without ever having seen her so much as play a card! Now that I look back on it, I believe she was also interested. The charming way in which she said "Not through the Iron Duke" as I played the second board should have made me suspect. However, Harold managed to pull himself together, and we succeeded in winning the duplicate with a 67.2 percent score. Mrs. Harris and Lucy were third, East and West.

Harold would not even go over the boards with me. As soon as the last card had been played, he was after me to introduce him to Lucy. I had no reason to refuse, and I brought them together directly after the scores were out. He wasted no time asking her for an opportunity to play bridge with her, and he was successful in his quest. Lucy was hardly to be rushed off her feet, of course, but she did promise him a Monday early in the succeeding month. He was like a man transported: It was a pleasure to look at him.

They played together when the day came, and soon they began to play together regularly. It was pleasant to watch them, for they made a lovely pair. Love had steadied Harold down; his psychics became less and less frequent and he was rebidding his cards as accurately as Culbertson himself, instead of wildly as had been his custom. Meanwhile, under his tutelage, Lucy was losing her weakness in squeezes and end-plays, and her opening leads had become things of beauty. They were consistent winners. And they were always together. I was with them when Harold first asked for her hand: She passed it to him and it was exactly what her bidding had indicated. It was all very idyllic.

As their bridge improved their love burgeoned. Here at the Club we were all in favor of it, knowing as we did that they would be odds-on favorites in the sectional Husband and Wife Tournament. Ultimately, we all were convinced that the announcements would be out as soon as our big tournament was completed, late in February, for they were planning to compete in it together and could hardly be expected to let anything else interfere. It was, I repeat, charming.

I pass lightly over the months that intervened before the big event. It came at last, and they qualified handily for the final round. I played with the club champion, and we were eliminated in the qualifying rounds, although I have been assured that during both sessions I had not so much as touched a wrong card. On one hand, holding the ace, jack and two small spades, three hearts to the queen, the diamond—I bet your pardon? Well, another time, perhaps. At any rate, we were eliminated, and for that reason I was able to follow Harold and Lucy in the finals.

They entered the round in second place, because of the carryover, but in a strong position. The lead was held by two youngsters whom none of us knew: They were far out in front but no one expected them to hold up through the pressure of a final round. Behind the two leading pairs the field was strung out evenly, with several strong teams still in the contention. It looked like a stirring finish.

But as the round wore along I realized, following Harold and Lucy, that they were almost certain to win.

Their game was rolling along smoothly and efficiently. On board seven Harold put in a brilliant bid, which I myself would scarcely have risen to, and they won a glorious score on the board. On board eleven Lucy delighted me with a double squeeze for another top. And at no time did they have a bad board: They were constantly average or better. Sixty-six percent was what I calculated, and I am not often wrong.

It was late in the session when they met the leaders. One look at the two boys was sufficient to convince me that the pressure was telling on them: They were pallid and worn, and as they took their cards out of the board their hands were trembling. I wonder if anyone but a bridge player can realize the strain that comes with a final round? The boys were showing every bit of it, and I felt sorry for them.

The first hand was uneventful. Lucy played the hand at three notrump, and although she attempted to set up an endplay she was able to take only nine tricks. However, the board was obviously flat, with no more than a point to be gained or lost by either side.

But the second board was a different story. Sitting behind Harold, I watched him wrestle with the bidding of the hand. He was faced with the problem which all tournament players dread: whether to bid three notrump on a hand and play it there, or to explore farther in a minor suit with an aim to investigating slam possibilities. Obviously, if the slam were not there and he chose to go beyond the three notrump level, he might find himself playing the hand at five diamonds, for a bad score. On the other hand, he suspected the slam, and was torn between the two courses of action. I struggled with him, and when he chose to go on, I suffered with him. Ultimately he bid six diamonds, and I held my breath as the dummy went down.

I might very well have sighed aloud with relief when I saw Lucy's hand. There were twelve tricks at diamonds, and only eleven at notrump; Lucy and Harold had put themselves into the perfect contract. All Harold had to do was lose a trick to the ace of trumps, draw the remaining trumps, and take the balance. Only a ruff could defeat him, and a ruff was most unlikely. It was perfection itself.

Harold won the opening lead, and returned a trump. On his left the boy showed out, but that made no difference, except to guarantee the contract. The other boy played a low trump, and Harold won the trick. He played another diamond, and much to his surprise the boy on his left, who had previously shown out, won the trick with the ace!

No one said anything for a moment, although we all were conscious of what had happened. Lucy broke the uncomfortable silence. "That was a revoke," she said. "You know your rights, partner?"

"I guess so," said Harold. "But it doesn't make any difference. We'll just forget it."

"Forget it!" exclaimed Lucy. "That was a revoke. We get that trick and another—if they take another."

"I have all the rest of the tricks," said Harold, "so we make six diamonds. As far as the revoke is concerned, I waive the penalty. Why should the kids lose the ace of trumps?"

"It's the rule," said Lucy. "A revoke is a revoke."

"Rule or no rule," said Harold. "I'm damned if I'll rub anything in. We have a good score on this board as it is, and when the day comes that the ace of trumps doesn't take a trick I'll quit the game."

At this point I informed Harold that his actions were contrary to the laws of duplicate. It was plainly stated, I told him, that in case of any infraction of the rules the tournament director must be called, and he must assign the proper penalty. There was no alternative, I pointed out.

"Listen here," said Harold. "These kids stand a chance of winning this event, and I won't see them lose it on a technicality. I won't call the director, and if anyone else does I'll claim that I didn't see any revoke. Or I'll revoke myself on the eleventh trick. Now let's get on with the tournament."

There was nothing we could do. The boys might have been able to rectify things, but they were new to tournament play in the first place, and in no condition to think clearly anyway. The move for the next round was called, and play went on.

But the sparkle was quite gone from Lucy and Harold's game. They were old campaigners, of course, and to the unpracticed observer all was as unruffled as ever, but the scores were hardly consistent as they had been, and there were no more tops. They finished up with two averages, and instead of going over their private score, as they usually did, they parted immediately. Harold disappeared to the bar, I believe, and Lucy came over to talk to me. "Do you realize what Harold did?" she said. "He cheated. He deliberately broke the rules." Of course I had no option but to agree with her. She walked away, her eyes flashing.

I need scarcely tell you that when the scores were posted, Harold's refusal to claim the revoke had cost three and a half points, and they had lost the event by two. The two boys had gone all to pieces and finished sixth, but another pair had come up and eked out the win. Warwick and Hutchins, to be precise. Harold and Lucy were second.

They never spoke to each other again. Lucy was heartbroken, but she was adamant. "I'm glad I found out in time," she told me one day. "He was a common cheat, and I never realized it."

I approached Harold about it one day, but he was brusque. "I don't wish to discuss it," he said, and though I brought it up time and again he walked away from me each time. Strangely enough, here in the Club the sympathy was mostly for Harold, although I remonstrated every chance I had, and even went so far as to read to several of the more stubborn sympathizers the rule in question.

Harold resigned from the Club soon after, and we heard little more of him. We did discover, however, that soon after he left, his true colors showed themselves again, and he took up a freak slam-bidding convention. He went from bad to worse, even dabbling with an artificial one-club system, and the last I heard he had given up bridge entirely after moving to another city.

Lucy was married shortly after, to an excellent bridge player from Philadelphia—a friend, I might add of Blackwood himself. She writes occasionally, never failing to mention her relief over having escaped so closely a marriage to so unscrupulous a man. She is happy, though scarcely rolling in wealth: Indeed, she is forced to run weekly duplicates in her home to eke out the family income. But in her last letter she tells me that her husband has promised to give up drinking, and that they stand a good chance of winning the National Mixed Pairs this spring.

"And so, gentlemen," concluded the Old Kibitzer, "I think you will agree that bridge can bring out a man's character."

"Let me ask you something," said the Underbidder. "What was that man's name again?"

"Harold Phillips," said the Kibitzer. "You know him?"

"I don't know," said the Underbidder. "Somehow the name sounds familiar."

"I can help you," said the Doubler. "You saw it in a newspaper. He was just made a Justice of the State Supreme Court—the youngest in history."

"Very likely," said the Old Kibitzer. "He was, as I said, a lawyer. But do not change the subject. Will you admit now, that bridge brings out a person's character?"

"I will," said the Doubler. "But don't press me for details!"

My Lady Love, My Dove

By Roald Dahl

IT HAS been my habit for many years to take a nap after lunch. I settle myself in a chair in the living room with a cushion behind my head and my feet up on a small square leather stool, and I read until I drop off.

On this Friday afternoon, I was in my chair and feeling as comfortable as ever with a book in my hands—an old favorite, Doubleday and Westwood's *The Genera of Diurnal Lepidoptera*—when my wife, who has never been a silent lady, began to talk to me from the sofa opposite. "These two people," she said, "what time are they coming?"

I made no answer, so she repeated the question, louder this time.

I told her politely that I didn't know.

"I don't think I like them very much," she said. "Especially him."

"No dear, all right."

"Arthur. I said I don't think I like them very much."

I lowered my book and looked across at her lying with her feet up on the sofa, flipping over the pages of some fashion magazine. "We've only met them once," I said.

"A dreadful man, really. Never stopped telling jokes, or stories, or something."

"I'm sure you'll manage them very well, dear."

"And she's pretty frightful, too. When do you think they'll arrive?"

Somewhere around six o'clock, I guessed.

"But don't *you* think they're awful?" she asked, pointing at me with her finger.

"Well . . ."

"They're *too* awful, they really are."

"We can hardly put them off now, Pamela."

"They're absolutely the end," she said.

"Then why did you ask them?" The question slipped out before I could stop myself and I regretted it at once, for it is a rule with me never to provoke my wife if I can help it. There was a pause, and I watched her face, waiting for the answer—the big white face that to me was something so strange and fascinating there were occasions when I could hardly bring myself to look away from it. In the evenings sometimes—working on her embroidery, or painting those small intricate flower pictures—the face would tighten and glimmer with a subtle inward strength that was beautiful beyond words, and I would sit and stare at it minute after minute while pretending to read. Even now, at this moment, with that compressed acid look, the frowning forehead, the petulant curl of the nose, I had to admit that there was a majestic quality about this woman, something splendid, almost stately; and so tall she was, far taller than I—although today, in her fifty-first year, I think one would have to call her big rather than tall.

"You know very well why I asked them," she answered sharply. "For bridge, that's all. They play an absolutely first-class game, and for a decent stake." She glanced up and saw me watching her. "Well," she said, "that's about the way you feel too, isn't it?"

"Well, of course, I . . ."

"Don't be a fool, Arthur."

"The only time I met them I must say they did seem quite nice."

"So is the butcher."

"Now Pamela, dear—please. We don't want any of that."

"Listen," she said, slapping down the magazine on her lap, "you saw the sort of people they were as well as I did. A pair of stupid climbers who think they can go anywhere just because they play good bridge."

"I'm sure you're right dear, but what I don't honestly understand is why—"

"I keep telling you—so that for once we can get a decent game. I'm sick and tired of playing with rabbits. But I really can't see why I should have these awful people in the house."

"Of course not, my dear, but isn't it a little late now—"

"Arthur?"

"Yes?"

"Why for God's sake do you always argue with me. You *know* you disliked them as much as I did."

"I really don't think you need worry, Pamela. After all, they seemed quite a nice well-mannered young couple."

"Arthur, don't be pompous." She was looking at me hard with those wide gray eyes of hers, and to avoid them —they sometimes made me quite uncomfortable—I got up and walked over to the French windows that led into the garden.

The big sloping lawn out in front of the house was newly mown, striped with pale and dark ribbons of green. On the far side, the two laburnums were in full flower at last, the long golden chains making a blaze of colour against the darker trees beyond. The roses were out too, and the scarlet begonias, and in the long herbaceous border all my lovely hybrid lupins, columbine, delphinium, sweet William, and the huge, pale, scented iris. One of the gardeners was coming up the drive from his lunch. I could see the roof of his cottage through the trees, and beyond it to one side, the place where the drive went out through the iron gates on the Canterbury road.

My wife's house. Her garden. How beautiful it all was! How peaceful! Now, if only Pamela would try to be a little less solicitous of my welfare, less prone to coax me into doing things for my own good rather than for my own pleasure, then everything would be heaven. Mind you, I don't want to give the impression that I do not love her—I worship the very air she breathes—or that I can't manage her, or that I am not the captain of my ship. All I am trying to say is that she can be a trifle irritating at times, the way she carries on. For example, those little mannerisms of hers—I do wish she would drop them all, especially the way she has of pointing a finger at me to emphasize a phrase. You must remember that I am a man who is built rather small, and a gesture like this, when used to excess by a person like my wife, is apt to intimidate. I sometimes find it difficult to convince myself that she is not an overbearing woman.

"Arthur!" she called. "Come here."

"What?"

"I've just had a most marvellous idea. Come here."

I turned and went over to where she was lying on the sofa.

"Look," she said, "do you want to have some fun?"

"What sort of fun?"

"With the Snapes."

"Who are the Snapes?"

"Come on," she said. "Wake up. Henry and Sally Snape. Our weekend guests."

"Well?"

"Now listen. I was lying here thinking how awful they really are . . . the way they behave . . . him with his jokes and her like a sort of love-crazed sparrow . . ." She hesitated, smiling slyly, and for some reason, I got the impression she was about to say a shocking thing. "Well—if that's the way they behave when they're in front of us, then what on earth must they be like when they're alone together?"

"Now wait a minute, Pamela—"

"Don't be an ass, Arthur. Let's have some fun—some real fun for once—tonight." She had half raised herself up off the sofa, her face bright with a kind of sudden recklessness, the mouth slightly open, and she was looking at me with two round gray eyes, a spark dancing slowly in each.

"Why shouldn't we?"

"What do you want to do?"

"Why, it's obvious. Can't you see?"

"No, I can't."

"All we've got to do is put a microphone in their room."

I admit I was expecting something pretty bad, but when she said this I was so shocked I didn't know what to answer.

"That's exactly what we'll do," she said.

"Here!" I cried. "No. Wait a minute. You can't do that."

"Why not?"

"That's about the nastiest trick I ever heard of. It's like—why, it's like listening at keyholes, or reading letters, only far far worse. You don't mean this seriously, do you?"

"Of course I do."

I knew how much she disliked being contradicted, but there were times when I felt it necessary to assert myself, even at considerable risk. "Pamela," I said, snapping the words out sharply, "I forbid you to do it!"

She took her feet down from the sofa and sat up straight. "What in God's name are you trying to pretend to be, Arthur? I simply don't understand you."

"That shouldn't be too difficult."

"Tommyrot! I've known you do lots of worse things than this before now."

"Never!"

"Oh yes I have. What makes you suddenly think you're a so much nicer person than I am?"

"I've never done things like that."

"All right my boy," she said, pointing her finger at me like a pistol. "What about that time at the Milfords' last Christmas? Remember? You nearly laughed your head off and I had to put my hand over your mouth to stop them hearing us. What about that for one?"

"That was different," I said. "It wasn't our house. And they weren't our guests."

"It doesn't make any difference at all." She was sitting very upright, staring at me with those round gray eyes, and the chin was beginning to come up high in a peculiarly contemptuous manner. "Don't be such a pompous hypocrite," she said. "What on earth's come over you?"

"I really think it's a pretty nasty thing, you know, Pamela. I honestly do."

"But listen, Arthur. I'm a *nasty* person. And so are you—in a secret sort of way. That's why we get along together."

"I never heard such nonsense."

"Mind you, if you've suddenly decided to change your character completely, that's another story."

"You've got to stop talking this way, Pamela."

"You see," she said, "if you really *have* decided to reform, then what on earth am I going to do?"

"You don't know what you're saying."

"Arthur, how could a nice person like you want to associate with a stinker?"

I sat myself down slowly in the chair opposite her, and she was watching me all the time. You understand, she was a big woman, with a big white face, and when she looked at me hard, as she was doing now, I became—how shall I say it—surrounded, almost enveloped by her, as though she were a great tub of cream and I had fallen in.

"You don't honestly want to do this microphone thing, do you?"

"But of course I do. It's time we had a bit of fun around here. Come on, Arthur. Don't be so stuffy."

"It's not right, Pamela."

"It's just as right"—up came the finger again—"just as right as when you found those letters of Mary Proberts' in her purse and you read them through from beginning to end."

"We should never have done that."

"*We!*"

"You read them afterwards, Pamela."

"It didn't harm anyone at all. You said so yourself at the time. And this one's no worse."

"How would *you* like it if someone did it to *you?*"

"How could I *mind* if I didn't know it was being done. Come on, Arthur. Don't be so flabby."

"I'll have to think about it."

"Maybe the great radio engineer doesn't know how to connect the mike to the speaker?"

"That's the easiest part."

"Well, go on then. Go on and do it."

"I'll think about it and let you know later."

"There's no time for that. They might arrive any moment."

"Then I won't do it. I'm not going to be caught red-handed."

"If they come before you're through, I'll simply keep them down here. No danger. What's the time anyway?"

It was nearly three o'clock.

"They're driving down from London," she said, "and they certainly won't leave till after lunch. That gives you plenty of time."

"Which room are you putting them in?"

"The big yellow room at the end of the corridor. That's not too far away, is it?"

"I suppose it could be done."

"And by the bye," she said, "where are you going to have the speaker?"

"I haven't said I'm going to do it yet."

"My God!" she cried, "I'd like to see someone try and stop you now. You ought to see your face. It's all pink and excited at the very prospect. Put the speaker in our bedroom, why not? But go on—and hurry."

I hesitated. It was something I made a point of doing whenever she tried to order me about, instead of asking nicely. "I don't like it, Pamela."

She didn't say any more after that; she just sat there, absolutely still, watching me, a resigned, waiting expression on her face, as though she were in a long queue. This, I knew from experience, was a danger signal. She was like one of those bomb things with the pin pulled out, and it was only a matter of time before—bang! and she would explode. In the silence that followed, I could almost hear her ticking.

So I got up quietly and went out to the workshop and collected a mike and a hundred and fifty feet of wire. Now that I was away from her, I am ashamed to admit that I began to feel a bit of excitement myself, a tiny warm prickling sensation under the skin, near the tips of my fingers. It was nothing much, mind you—really nothing at all. Good heavens, I experience the same thing every morning of my life when I open the paper to check the closing prices on two or three of my wife's larger stockholdings. So I wasn't going to get carried away by a silly joke like this. At the same time, I couldn't help being amused.

I took the stairs two at a time and entered the yellow room at the end of the passage. It had the clean, unlived-in appearance of all guest rooms, with its twin beds, yellow satin bedspreads, pale-yellow walls, and golden-colored curtains. I began to look around for a good place to hide the mike. This was the most important part of all, for whatever happened, it must not be discovered. I thought first of the basket of logs by the fireplace. Put it under the logs. No—not safe enough. Behind the radiator? On top of the wardrobe? Under the desk? None of these seemed very professional to me. All might be subject to chance inspection because of a dropped collar stud or something like that. Finally, with considerable cunning, I decided to put it inside of the springing of the sofa. The sofa was against the wall, near the edge of the carpet, and my lead wire could go straight under the carpet over to the door.

I tipped up the sofa and slit the material underneath. Then I tied the microphone securely up among the springs, making sure that it faced the room. After that, I led the wire under the carpet to the door. I was calm and cautious in everything I did. Where the wire had to emerge from under the carpet and pass out of the door, I made a little groove in the wood so that it was almost invisible.

All this, of course, took time, and when I suddenly heard the crunch of wheels on the gravel of the drive outside, and then the slamming of car doors and the voices of our guests, I was still only halfway down the corridor, tacking the wire along the skirting. I stopped and straightened up, hammer in hand, and I must confess that I felt afraid. You have no idea how unnerving that noise was to me. I experienced the same sudden stomachy feeling of fright as when a bomb once dropped the other side of the village during the war, one afternoon, while I was working quietly in the library with my butterflies.

Don't worry, I told myself. Pamela will take care of these people. She won't let them come up here.

Rather frantically, I set about finishing the job, and soon I had the wire tacked all along the corridor and through into our bedroom. Here, concealment was not so important, although I still did not permit myself to get careless because of the servants. So I laid the wire under the carpet and brought it up unobtrusively into the back of the radio. Making the final connections was an elementary technical matter and took me no time at all.

Well—I had done it. I stepped back and glanced at the little radio. Somehow, now, it looked different—no longer a silly box for making noises but an evil little creature that crouched on the tabletop with a part of its own body reaching out secretly into a forbidden place far away. I switched it on. It hummed faintly but made no other sound. I took my bedside clock, which had a loud tick, and carried it along to the yellow room and placed it on the floor by the sofa. When I returned, sure enough the radio creature was ticking away as loudly as if the clock were in the room—even louder.

I fetched back the clock. Then I tidied myself up in the bathroom, returned my tools to the workshop, and prepared to meet the guests. But first, to compose myself, and so that I would not have to appear in front of them with the blood, as it were, still wet on my hands, I spent five minutes in the library with my collection. I concentrated on a tray of the lovely *Vanessa cardui*—the "painted lady"—and made a few notes for a paper I was preparing entitled "The Relation between Color Pattern and Framework of Wings," which I intended to read at the next meeting of our society in Canterbury. In this way I soon regained my normal grave, attentive manner.

When I entered the living room, our two guests, whose names I could never remember, were seated on the sofa. My wife was mixing drinks.

"Oh, *there* you are, Arthur," she said. "Where *have* you been?"

I thought this was an unnecessary remark. "I'm so sorry," I said to the guests as we shook hands. "I was busy and forgot the time."

"We all know what *you've* been doing," the girl said, smiling wisely. "But we'll forgive him, won't we, dearest?"

"I think we should," the husband answered.

I had a frightful, fantastic vision of my wife telling them, amidst roars of laughter, precisely what I had been doing upstairs. She *couldn't*—she *couldn't* have done that! I looked round at her and she too was smiling as she measured out the gin.

"I'm sorry we disturbed you," the girl said.

I decided that if this was going to be a joke then I'd

better join in quickly, so I forced myself to smile with her.

"You must let us see it," the girl continued.

"See what?"

"Your collection. Your wife says that they are absolutely beautiful."

I lowered myself slowly into a chair and relaxed. It was ridiculous to be so nervous and jumpy. "Are you interested in butterflies?" I asked her.

"I'd love to see yours, Mr. Beauchamp."

The Martinis were distributed and we settled down to a couple of hours of talk and drink before dinner. It was from then on that I began to form the impression that our guests were a charming couple. My wife, coming from a titled family, is apt to be conscious of her class and breeding, and is often hasty in her judgment of strangers who are friendly toward her—particularly tall men. She is frequently right, but in this case I felt that she might be making a mistake. As a rule, I myself do not like tall men either; they are apt to be supercilious and omniscient. But Henry Snape—my wife had whispered his name—struck me as being an amiable simple young man with good manners whose main preoccupation, very properly, was Mrs. Snape. He was handsome in a long-faced, horsy sort of way, with dark-brown eyes that seemed to be gentle and sympathetic. I envied him his fine mop of black hair, and caught myself wondering what lotion he used to keep it looking so healthy. He did tell us one or two jokes, but they were on a high level and no one could have objected.

"At school," he said, "they used to call me Scervix. Do you know why?"

"I haven't the least idea," my wife answered.

"Because cervix is Latin for nape."

This was rather deep and it took me a while to work out.

"What school was that, Mr. Snape?" my wife asked.

"Eton," he said, and my wife gave a quick little nod of approval. Now she will talk to him, I thought, so I turned my attention to the other one, Sally Snape. She was an attractive girl with a bosom. Had I met her fifteen years earlier I might well have gotten myself into some sort of trouble. As it was, I had a pleasant enough time telling her all about my beautiful butterflies. I was observing her closely as I talked, and after a while I began to get the impression that she was not, in fact, quite so merry and smiling a girl as I had been led to believe at first. She seemed to be coiled in herself, as though with a secret she was jealously guarding. The deep-blue eyes moved too quickly about the room, never settling or resting on one thing for more than a moment; and over all her face, though so faint that they might not even have been there, those small downward lines of sorrow.

"I'm so looking forward to our game of bridge," I said finally changing the subject.

"Us too," she answered. "You know we play almost every night, we love it so."

"You are extremely expert, both of you. How did you get to be so good?"

"It's practice," she said. "That's all. Practice, practice, practice."

"Have you played in any championships?"

"Not yet, but Henry wants very much for us to do that. It's hard work, you know, to reach that standard. Terribly hard work." Was there not here, I wondered, a hint of resignation in her voice? Yes, that was probably it; he was pushing her too hard, making her take it too seriously, and the poor girl was tired of it all.

At eight o'clock, without changing, we moved in to dinner. The meal went well, with Henry Snape telling us some very droll stories. He also praised my Richebourg '34 in a most knowledgeable fashion, which pleased me greatly. By the time coffee came, I realized that I had grown to like these two youngsters immensely, and as a result I began to feel uncomfortable about this microphone business. It would have been all right if they had been horrid people, but to play this trick on two such charming young persons as these filled me with a strong sense of guilt. Don't misunderstand me. I was not getting cold feet. It didn't seem necessary to stop the operation. But I refused to relish the prospect openly as my wife seemed now to be doing, with covert smiles and winks and secret little noddings of the head.

Around nine thirty, feeling comfortable and well fed, we returned to the large living room to start our bridge. We were playing for a fair stake—ten shillings a hundred—so we decided not to split families, and I partnered my wife the whole time. We all four of us took the game seriously, which is the only way to take it, and we played silently, intently, hardly speaking at all except to bid. It was not the money we played for. Heaven knows, my wife had enough of that, and so apparently did the Snapes. But among experts it is almost traditional that they play for a reasonable stake.

That night the cards were evenly divided, but for once my wife played badly, so we got the worst of it. I could see that she wasn't concentrating fully, and as we came along toward midnight she began not even to care. She kept glancing up at me with those large gray eyes of hers, the eyebrows raised, the nostrils curiously open, a little gloating smile around the corners of her mouth.

Our opponents played a fine game. Their bidding was masterly, and all through the evening they made only one mistake. That was when the girl badly overestimated her partner's hand and bid six spades. I doubled and they went three down, vulnerable, which cost them eight hundred points. It was just a momentary lapse, but I remember that Sally Snape was very put out by it, even though her husband forgave her at once, kissing her hand across the table and telling her not to worry.

Around twelve thirty my wife announced that she wanted to go to bed.

"Just one more rubber?" Henry Snape said.

"No, Mr. Snape. I'm tired tonight. Arthur's tired, too. I can see it. Let's all go to bed."

She herded us out of the room and we went upstairs, the four of us together. On the way up, there was the usual talk about breakfast and what they wanted and how they were to call the maid. "I think you'll like your room," my wife said. "It has a view right across the valley, and the sun comes to you in the morning around ten o'clock."

We were in the passage now, standing outside our own bedroom door, and I could see the wire I had put down that afternoon and how it ran along the top of the skirting down to their room. Although it was nearly the same color as the paint, it looked very conspicuous to me. "Sleep well," my wife said. "Sleep well, Mrs. Snape. Good night, Mr. Snape." I followed her into our room and shut the door.

"Quick!" she cried. "Turn it on!" My wife was always like that, frightened that she was going to miss something. She had a reputation, when she went hunting—I never go myself—of always being right up with the hounds whatever the cost to herself or her horse for fear that she might miss a kill. I could see she had no intention of missing this one.

The little radio warmed up just in time to catch the

noise of their door opening and closing again.

"There!" my wife said. "They've gone in." She was standing in the center of the room in her blue dress, her hands clasped before her, her head craned forward, intently listening, and the whole of the big white face seemed somehow to have gathered itself together, tight like a wineskin.

Almost at once the voice of Henry Snape came out of the radio, strong and clear. "You're just a goddam little fool," he was saying, and this voice was so different from the one I remembered, so harsh and unpleasant, it made me jump. "The whole bloody evening wasted! Eight hundred points—that's four pounds!"

"I got mixed up," the girl answered. "I won't do it again, I promise."

"What's *this?*" my wife said. "What's going on?" Her mouth was wide open now, the eyebrows stretched up high, and she came quickly over to the radio and leaned forward, ear to the speaker. I must say I felt rather excited myself.

"I promise, I promise I won't do it again," the girl was saying.

"We're not taking any chances," the man answered grimly. "We're going to have another practice right now."

"Oh no, please! I couldn't stand it!"

"Look," the man said, "all the way out here to take money off this rich bitch and you have to go and mess it up."

My wife's turn to jump.

"The second time this week," he went on.

"I promise I won't do it again."

"Sit down. I'll sing them out and you answer."

"No, Henry, *please!* Not all five hundred of them. It'll take three hours."

"All right, then. We'll leave out the finger positions. I think you're sure of those. We'll just do the basic bids showing honor tricks."

"Oh, Henry, must we? I'm so tired."

"It's absolutely essential you get them perfect," he said. "We have a game every day next week, you know that. And we've got to eat."

"What is this?" my wife whispered. "What on earth is it?"

"Shhh!" I said. "Listen."

"All right," the man's voice was saying. "Now we'll start from the beginning. Ready?"

"Oh Henry, *please*." She sounded very near to tears.

"Come on, Sally. Pull yourself together."

Then, in a quite different voice, the one we had been used to hearing in the living room, Henry Snape said, "*One* club." I noticed that there was a curious lilting emphasis on the word "one," the first part of the word drawn out long.

"Ace queen of clubs," the girl replied wearily. "King jack of spades. No hearts, and ace jack of diamonds."

"And how many cards to each suit? Watch my finger positions carefully."

"You said we could miss those."

"Well—if you're quite sure you know them?"

"Yes, I know them."

A pause, then "A *club*."

"King jack of clubs," the girl recited. "Ace of spades. Queen jack of hearts, and ace queen of diamonds."

Another pause, then "I'll say *one* club."

"Ace king of clubs . . ."

"My heavens alive!" I cried. "It's a bidding code! They show every card in the hand!"

"Arthur, it couldn't be!"

"It's like those men who go into the audience and borrow something from you and there's a girl blindfolded on the stage, and from the way he phrases the question she can tell him exactly what it is—even a railway ticket, and what station it's from."

"It's impossible!"

"Not at all. But it's tremendous hard work to learn. Listen to them."

"I'll go *one heart*," the man's voice was saying.

"King queen ten of hearts. Ace jack of spades. No diamonds. Queen jack of clubs . . ."

"And you see," I said, "he tells her the *number* of cards he has in each suit by the position of his fingers."

"How?"

"I don't know. You heard him saying about it."

"My *God*, Arthur! Are you sure that's what they're doing?"

"I'm afraid so." I watched her as she walked quickly over to the side of the bed to fetch a cigarette. She lit it with her back to me and then swung round, blowing the smoke up at the ceiling in a thin stream. I knew we were going to have to do something about this, but I wasn't quite sure what because we couldn't possibly accuse them without revealing the source of our information. I waited for my wife's decision.

"Why, Arthur," she said slowly, blowing out clouds of smoke. "Why, this is a *mar-vellous* idea. D'you think *we* could learn to do it?"

"What!"

"Of course. Why not?"

"Here! No! Wait a minute, Pamela . . ." But she came swiftly across the room, right up close to me where I was standing, and she dropped her head and looked down at me—the old look of a smile that wasn't a smile, at the corners of the mouth, and the curl of the nose, and the big full gray eyes staring at me with their bright black centers, and then they were gray, and all the rest was white flecked with hundreds of tiny red veins—and when she looked at me like this, hard and close, I swear to you it made me feel as though I were drowning.

"Yes," she said. "Why not?"

"But Pamela . . . Good heavens . . . No . . . After all . . ."

"Arthur, I do wish you wouldn't *argue* with me all the time. That's exactly what we'll do. Now, go fetch a deck of cards; we'll start right away."

The Great Kibitzers' Strike of 1926

By George S. Kaufman

SINCE I was a close observer of events leading up to the national strike of bridge kibitzers some years ago, and subsequently a member of the committee that helped to bring about a settlement, I think it is fitting for me to set down the true story of those turbulent days. There has long been a belief that the trouble started when a kibitzer named Lefkowitz—not Sam Lefkowitz, who later demanded that kibitzers be allowed to double any slam contract, but a cousin of his, named Marty—applied a hotfoot to a player during a six-no-trump contract. The Lefkowitz hotfoot case was not without its points of interest, and the depositions taken in the hospital are now preserved in the Library of Congress, but it was not the cause of the kibitzers' strike.

On the night of May 12, 1926, in the old Cavendish Club, on East Sixty-fifth Street, a player named Jymes, or Hymes, or something—the records are unfortunately vague—concealed a queen of spades from a kibitzer, known simply as Commander Smith, during the play of a hand. By holding the spade queen behind the four of diamonds, Jymes completely confused the kibitzer in his calculations, leading him to believe that he would make only three spades instead of four. Since this was during the old game of auction, before contract became popular, not a great deal was thought about it at the moment, and nothing was said. Smith himself stayed in his place for the rest of the evening, but it was noticed when the game broke up that he failed to ask, "What time are you boys playing tomorrow?"

On the following night, Smith didn't show up. It was the first night he had missed in eleven years, but still no one was worried; it was simply assumed that he was dead. This had happened before to kibitzers, and the procedure in such cases was well established. One of the players would deal and say, "Did you notice that Bill Clunk died last night? One spade," and his partner, when it came to his turn, would say, "Yes, I did. Two spades." Or diamonds, or hearts, or whatever it might be. So the players would kitty out three dollars for flowers, and that would be that. (How times have changed! Under today's rules, the death of a kibitzer calls for the cessation of play for a full ten seconds, and the next four hands are automatically doubled.)

But to get back to Smith, when the next day's papers carried no obituary notice, the players began to be worried. That evening, Smith was absent again, and this time one of the players put in a phone call to Smith's house. Smith was home, reading a book! Not a bridge book, either—some sort of novel. The fat was in the fire for fair!

The following night, two more kibitzers were missing, and from then on the thing grew by leaps and bounds. Smith held an indignation meeting at his home on the fourth night, with nearly fifty kibitzers in attendance. Subcommittees were formed and chairmen were appointed in Queens and the Bronx; inside of three weeks there was not a kibitzer on duty in Greater New York. Picketing was started in front of the Knickerbocker Whist Club, and a rock was shied at Oswald Jacoby's head as he was entering the club. Happily, it hit an old lady who was not even a bridge player.

There was, of course, consternation within the clubs. With no kibitzer to say, "You should have played it the other way around" or "Only a fathead would have led the king of diamonds," post-mortem discussions were routine and without color. Without kibitzers, the players became careless and listless; games simply dragged along, sometimes without comment of any sort. The players began to lose weight, had no appetites. In many cases, games were actually cancelled.

Jymes, or Hymes, or whatever his name was, eventually offered public apology to Smith for concealing the spade queen, but by then it was too late. Sympathy strikes were springing up all over the country, a national kibitzers' union was formed, and cardplayers were presented with an ultimatum in the form of a set of rules. Among the stipulations were these:

Recognition of the union as the only bargaining force for kibitzers, and an agreement that no game should be started without at least two kibitzers in attendance.

Cessation of play if a kibitzer was called to the telephone.

The right of the kibitzer to call a revoke if it was confirmed by another kibitzer.

If a kibitzer had to go home before the end of the game, the results were to be telephoned to him as soon as the game was over.

The right of the kibitzer to put his glass of water on the bridge table.

And many others.

Negotiations were deadlocked for four months, and in that time there were many outbreaks of violence and sabotage. In a Minneapolis bridge club, the six of clubs exploded in a player's hand, and was found afterward to have been dusted with TNT. In Dallas, a deck of cards was found to have three aces of spades in it, and this crime was traced to a kibitzer who had managed to get a job in a card factory. In New York City, fifteen thousand kibitzers held an indignation meeting in Union Square, and many were beaten by the police when they tried to parade without a permit. In the ensuing riot, three people were trampled to death. In Seattle, a player who went down one on a cold slam claimed that he had been quietly given a needle by a kibitzer who had jostled him on the sidewalk. Ely Culbertson was burned in effigy.

On September 28th, President Coolidge appealed to both sides to settle the controversy before there was further property damage or loss of life. Leaders of the two factions assembled in the White House on October 9th, and on the night of October 22nd, at a little after ten o'clock, the formal announcement of peace was made. I do not want to claim too much credit for the settlement, but when the conference had been deadlocked three days over the question of penalties for a kibitzer's foot on a player's chair, it was I who suggested a happy compromise. The foot, I said, should be amputated, not burned off.

The Adventure of the Panamanian Girls

By Frank Thomas

When, according to the will of John H. Watson, M.D., the famous dispatch box which had rested so long in the vaults of Cox's Bank at Charing Cross was finally opened, the world was astounded to learn that Sherlock Holmes, master of deduction, was also a bridge player. In "Sherlock Holmes, Bridge Detective," the story of how Watson taught Holmes the game and how they became involved in "The Challenge Match" against politician Harry Skurry and his partner, Betty Castle, is revealed in detail. In his "Diary of the Challenge Match," Doctor Watson felt strongly that Holmes, in the singular affair of the Panamanian Girls, was at his peak, not only as a detective but as a bridge player and theorist.

THE weather had mellowed somewhat in London at this time, a fact which pleased Doctor Watson. He worried about Holmes since the detective had been under tremendous strain. Not only did his Challenge Match exploits occupy his time, but Holmes had just brought to a conclusion the matter of the Netherland-Sumatra

Company and the colossal schemes of Baron Maupertuis. (See: "The Reigate Squires.") Watson felt at this time that a continuation of the Match might be injurious to his friend's health. To play as a mere novice is one thing, but now Holmes was hailed on all sides as a great bridge innovator and master strategist. His every move at the table was carefully watched by an army of kibitzers, which had to produce some inner tension, even to as cool a hand as Holmes.

Of course, the Netherland-Sumatra case was one of the highpoints in Holmes' lifelong battle against crime. He had succeeded where the police of three countries had failed. Europe was ringing with his name and 221B Baker Street was ankle-deep with congratulatory telegrams.

At this point, a most opportune invitation was extended to the participants in the Challenge Match. England's most avid bridge buff, the Duke of Cumberland, invited the players to vacate the Grosvenor Square Club for a week and play the Challenge Match at his favorite bridge club in Bath. Bridge was played by all of the high society who frequented this luxurious gaming resort and they were eager to be able to observe the match which was, by now, the talk of London and, indeed, all of England.

Watson felt that a trip from London and a change of scene would be beneficial to Holmes, but he was in serious doubts as to the detective agreeing to the idea. Holmes shunned mass adulation, and the idea of playing in one of Bath's historical gaming rooms surrounded by those who had no interest in the Challenge Match at its outset would, in Watson's opinion, strike Holmes as repugnant. Betty Castle and Harry Skurry were ecstatic when the idea was first broached. What lady of fashion or politician would not warmly embrace an invitation from such an illustrious nobleman? But Holmes was cut from different cloth, as proven by his rejection of knighthood following the affair of "The Marzarin Stone."

Much to the concerned Watson's surprise, Holmes fell in with the idea of the week's change in locale quite readily. The Duke was notified that the four contestants were delighted to accept his invitation and arrangements were made for the group to entrain for Bath from Liverpool Station.

But now a hue and cry arose from the loyal followers at the Grosvenor Club. Their contention was that the match, which they had followed and supported, might very well be settled one way or another in a week's play. The London journals, which had made great copy from the contest, joined forces with the rebellious bridge addicts. To calm the furor, the Duke magnanimously offered to charter a special train to bring the contestants and a large number of kibitzers to Bath. This gesture overwhelmed opposition, but gave the whole undertaking a holiday and somewhat circus-atmosphere. Again, Watson was fearful that Holmes would withdraw from the project, but the sleuth stood by his word.

It was on a Saturday afternoon that "The Challenge Match Express," loaded with actual and would-be bridgeplayers, roared out of Liverpool Station to the stirring notes of a brass band provided by The Northumberland Fusiliers, Watson's old regiment.

Holmes was patiently cordial through all the fanfare and farewells but during the trip kept to himself as much as possible going over an extensive sheaf of newspaper clippings which he had removed from his voluminous files prior to departure. This caused the good doctor to take another view towards his friend's behavior. Holmes, if he was capable of the emotion at all, feared the reaction which historically followed the completion of a major case and habitually made him prey to the blackest depression. Nothing pleased him more than to have another matter to tease his intellect. It crossed Watson's mind that, quite possibly, something was brewing in Bath other than bridge.

Upon its arrival in Bath, the special train was met at the station by the Duke and a large group. Sir Henry Irving, one of England's foremost actors, delivered the "Once More Into The Breach" speech from "Henry, the Fifth."

Through it all, Holmes had a preoccupied air. Finally, arrangements for lodgings were made and it was agreed that the contestants would play for half a day beginning at one P.M., Sunday. Play would continue through the following week, terminating on Friday. The crowd dispersed in various directions and it was now that the idea which had been flitting around the edge of Watson's brain crystallized into fact. Holmes headed purposefully for the Bath Police Station.

At the home of the local constabulary, Holmes was greeted warmly and gratefully by Chief Constable Fenwick Trescott, a youngish man with a frank and open manner.

"I'm delighted that you could respond to my telegram, Mr. Holmes," said the Chief Constable, after introductions were made. "How fortunate for me that you could bring Doctor Watson with you."

Watson, who never considered himself an asset in mat-

NOTE: It should be mentioned that the Duke of Cumberland could well afford to import the contestants in the Challenge Match plus followers. It was this very same Duke who, later, in Bath, lost twenty thousand pounds on one hand of Bridge! In modern currency (American), this amounts to around half a million dollars. Known as "The Duke of Cumberland Hand" it is probably the most famous deal in the history of bridge, but that is another story.

ters of criminology, offered the comment that both their presences were needed for the bridge match.

"Bridge?" said Trescott, with a puzzled look. "What's that?"

Holmes looked at him sharply. "Nothing but a game, Trescott, but one you might well consider learning. It is an excellent exercise in the subtle art of deduction."

"If you say so, sir, that's good enough for me. You might say I have a restricted choice." Trescott indicated Dr. Watson. "Does your associate know of our trouble down here?"

Holmes gestured negatively. "I have found it useful for Dr. Watson to have a clear mind on many cases. Besides, I would like to hear of the incident in your own words."

Trescott obliged.

"A recent resident, one John Ehrlenvale, caused quite a local stir by purchasing one of the Panamanian Girl paintings by Edward Henry Lansing. Ehrlenvale made a pile in tea in Ceylon and bought one of our largest showplaces here. He secured the picture from another local resident, Lord Duncan whom you know about, Mr. Holmes."

As the detective nodded, Trescott continued, centering on Dr. Watson.

"At the time of the purchase, I received a wire from Mr. Holmes cautioning me that the Panamanian Girl paintings had a habit of disappearing." His eyes swiveled to Holmes. "I had my men watch the Ehrlenvale residence closely, but when it was done, it was done smooth as silk: a window forced, a bolt sawed through, and the painting gone. That's when I wired you, Mr. Holmes. Ehrlenvale has been kicking up a fearful row." A tinge of satisfaction touched the chief constable's face. "But there's been a break in the case, sir. A constable noted a man at the railway station who looked familiar and he took him into custody. It was Oswald Sacker, a name familiar to you, Mr. Holmes."

"You did make a catch," said Holmes. For Watson's benefit, he added: "One of the most notorious cracksmen in England with a record that would fill a book."

"He has no explanation for his presence in Bath," continued Trescott. "And he won't admit to anything. Actually, we're straining things a bit keeping him in custody since we have no actual proof."

"No indication of what he might have done with the painting?"

Trescott shook his head.

"No burglar tools in his possession naturally?"

"No, sir. As I say, it was purely by chance that he was picked up at all. One strange thing though was his shoes."

Holmes was immediately alert and Watson knew why. It was a contention of the sleuth that shoes were a most overlooked source of clues. Many times, Watson had heard his friend state: "Shoes often indicate where one is going and show where one has been."

"What about Sacker's shoes?" asked Holmes.

"They had a lot of ash on them. Naturally, I went over everything he was wearing, closely. I was struck by the ashes that had adhered to the soles and heels of his boots."

At Holmes' request, Trescott secured the shoes of the cracksman and the detective studied them carefully with his ever-present pocket glass.

"Hmmmm," he mumbled. "We'd better get these to your laboratory."

Trescott colored slightly. "This isn't quite like London, sir. A police laboratory is something we just don't have."

"All I need is a powerful microscope," said Holmes, hopefully, but Trescott shook his head.

"I say, Holmes, a doctor might be able to fill the bill." Watson was glad to be able to contribute to the conversation.

"What an excellent idea, my dear Watson."

It was arranged that Trescott would attempt to secure the needed equipment and have it ready for Holmes' trained eye on the following morning.

Night time was upon them and Holmes and Watson were taken to "The Fox and The Crown," the local inn at which they were staying, by dog cart. Discussion was postponed until they enjoyed an excellent meal in the suite at their disposal. Then Holmes lit his pipe and sank into a large chair. Through a cloud of smoke, he regarded Watson humorously.

"We're a long way from bridge, eh, old boy?"

"And I am as mystified as usual," admitted Watson ruefully. "The paintings referred to and their creator are just vaguely familiar to me."

"A knowledge gap which I would share," said Holmes, "but for the fact that the singular history of the Panamanian Girls has been fascinating me for several years. Hence, the sheaf of clippings which I brought with me on the train."

"I noticed," said Watson proudly.

"I noticed you noticing," said Holmes. "Let me fill you in on the results of my research to date."

"The story begins almost fifty years ago. Edward Henry Lansing was a British painter who attracted no notice whatever until a modest inheritance from an uncle allowed him to fulfill a dream and visit Panama. What his reason was to go to this far-off and most uncivilized area we shall never know. He lived there for two years and then returned to England. Evidently, his artistic soul was inspired by the vivid colors, the striking contrasts of the tropics. On his return, he painted four great oils, each one considered a masterpiece. The four Panamanian Girls. He created these paintings at an amazing rate, as if under compulsion."

"Perhaps inspired by some native girl?" interjected Watson slyly.

"A possibility," said Holmes, "but an unrecorded one. In any case, his paintings received immediate acclaim. His vivid colors dazzled art critics. In later years, his work was presumed to have inspired both Van Gogh and Gauguin. It was said that one of the Panamanian Girl paintings would light up a dark room. Obviously an impossibility, but quite expressive, don't you think?"

"Indeed," agreed Watson. "Please continue Holmes. This is absolutely fascinating."

"Most stories full of conjecture are," replied the detective dryly. "One can imagine any number of answers to all the unsolved questions. What drove Lansing to Panama? What transformed him from an unknown painter into a genius in two years? What inspired him to create four masterpieces all with the same name and the same general subject? We don't know because with the acclaim of the world of art ringing in his ears, Edward Henry Lansing died as the result of a fever contracted in the tropics. That's one of the reasons his name is only vaguely familiar to you."

"Your tone indicates there may be another reason," hazarded Watson shrewdly.

"Touché," replied Holmes. "Over thirty years ago, when the financial state of England and the continent was at a momentary low ebb, Lord Henry Duncan was able to purchase all four of the Lansing paintings. It was a wise time to buy art but it is said that Lord Duncan bankrupt his considerable family fortune to secure the Panamanian Girls."

"A rash speculation," said Watson.

"If a speculation at all," continued Holmes. "Shortly after securing the paintings, Lord Duncan and his wife were estranged and she went to live and die in the south of France. It created quite a scandal at the time, but Duncan's name was never associated with another woman and the gossip subsided. When he died, the estate passed to the only offspring, the present Lord Duncan. His inheritance consisted of a heavily mortgaged castle and a mountain of debts and, of course, the Panamanian Girls. But they remained hanging in Duncan Castle, unseen by the general public, for a quarter of a century. Finally, five years ago, the present Lord Duncan sold one of them to Victor Selkirk."

"At least, one of the paintings was back in circulation."

"Hardly," replied Holmes. "Two months after the purchase, Selkirk's mansion caught fire. The painting was destroyed, along with Mr. Selkirk. Then, three years ago, Lord Duncan sold the second Panamanian Girl to one J. C. Grimes. It was stolen. And it's never been found."

"Good heavens, Holmes! What a weird history! It's almost as though there was a curse on those paintings."

"If one believed in such things," replied the detective. "Especially, since the third Panamanian Girl went to an industrialist in the Midlands. It disappeared under very suspicious circumstances. The contention was the painting was inexplicably lost in transit. There was a law suit about it and Lord Duncan won a settlement of one-half of the agreed price."

"From the way your story goes, I'm sure the painting was never found."

"Quite right, Watson. And now you know as much as I do. If our suspicions are correct, the fourth and last Panamanian Girl has disappeared."

Watson regarded his old friend with wondrous eyes. "Holmes, this must be one of the strangest cases of your career."

"I'll concede that the background is a trifle exotic," said the detective. "However, the solution is so simple that it hardly ranks as a case at all. The clues are the strange effect those four paintings had on certain people. Consider the actions of the former and the present Lord Duncan. Duncan père, an otherwise sane nobleman of the period, dissipated his considerable fortune and wrecked his marriage just to possess the four paintings. The son never married and has lived for years in semi-poverty but tenaciously holding on to the Panamanian Girls. I recall the words of one of the first art critics to laud the Lansing paintings. In writing of them, the man was almost hysterical in his description of the . . ."

Holmes paused for a moment, and then quoted: " 'Incomparable beauty of the Panamanian Girls. . . . Four native Eves set against the lush background of a tropical Eden.' "

Watson stroked his moustache nervously. "Heavens, Holmes, you don't mean that men actually fell in love with the paintings—the Duncans and others, I mean? Well, dash it . . . !"

"You have it, Watson," exclaimed Holmes. " 'And others' is the key. Obviously, Lansing's masterful paintings did produce a profound effect. Suppose you were a devotee of the Lansing works cursed with an obsession to have them for your own—not for display or sale, but as a possession. You attempt to buy them but perhaps the price is too steep. The one is sold to Victor Selkirk, a rather coarse man as I understand it and but recently come to great wealth. You steal the painting and set fire to the Selkirk mansion. Ostensibly, the painting is no more, but actually you have it."

"But what about the others?" asked Watson. "Grimes' painting and the one here in Bath that Ehrlenvale purchased?"

"Those were outright thefts," admitted the detective, "with no attempt at concealment. However, when the Selkirk mansion was destroyed, all within perished in the fire. Possibly, this wholesale slaughter was too much for the man behind the scheme."

Holmes knocked ashes from the bowl of his pipe.

"No, Watson, I rather imagine the solution to this problem will be routine police work. A man with an obsession is not hard to find. You will recall that even Moriarty could not resist hanging that Greuze painting behind his desk."

Holmes rose from his easy chair. "The mystery of the Panamanian Girls is but a few loose ends from solution, I believe. But there is still the Challenge Match to be dealt with. We'd better get some sleep."

"We are in the lead," said Watson, with satisfaction.

"Leads, in anything, can be very temporary," stated Holmes. After a moment, he added: "Opening leads are a constant frustration." This bit of philosophy was the end of their discussion for the night.

The following morning found Holmes and Watson at the Bath Police Station. Chief Constable Trescott had been able to secure an excellent microscope which brought a gleam to Holmes' eyes. A certain Doctor Theodore Laughtner of Bath provided it along with some other items which Holmes needed. Armed with his temporary equipment, the great consulting detective went to work. After better than an hour of exhaustive tests of Sacker's shoes, Holmes was ready with his findings. However, his face was tense, and his confident manner had disappeared.

"Ashes, to the untrained eye, all look alike. But in actuality, they can be of hundreds of different varieties."

Trescott was eagerly following the detective's words. "I read your monograph on cigar ashes with great interest, Mr. Holmes."

Holmes paused for a grateful smile. Trescott's single sentence probably meant more to him than an accolade from Parliament.

"The ashes on Sacker's shoes were certainly not from tobacco," he continued. "They showed traces of wood as well as of canvas of considerable age." Holmes delivered his next sentence with a sad note. "The ashes also revealed paint. I would say artist paint, also of considerable age."

Trescott's eyes widened as Watson burst out explosively: "Good heavens, Holmes, you can't mean . . . !"

The detective nodded. "On the meager evidence at hand, I give you the following *prima facie* case: Sacker stole the Panamanian Girl painting from the Ehrlenvale mansion, an assumption based on his record. On leaving with the painting, he disposed of whatever tools he used in the burglary and somewhere burned the painting, stamping on the fire at times to prevent its growing large enough to attract attention." A sudden thought struck him. "Trescott, when the painting was stolen, was the frame taken as well?"

The Chief Constable, still somewhat in shock, just nodded.

"Hence the traces of wood ashes," continued Holmes.

He rose to his feet. "It would do me no good to see Oswald Sacker. He's an old lag and nothing will crack him except absolute evidence. Doctor Watson and I are due for the afternoon session of play in the Challenge Match, but the next step is up to you, Trescott, in any case."

The Chief Constable's eyes pleaded for more guidance, so Holmes elaborated: "Sacker was at the Ehrlenvale mansion, a reasonable assumption. Sacker was at the railway station, where your man spotted him, which is a fact. Somewhere between these two points there must be the remains of a small fire. Probably concealed, but your task is simplified by the fact that there are just so many locations, where a fire may be set without arousing unwanted curiosity. I imagine this search will strain your available manpower, but I'm sure you realize the necessity of haste."

"I do, indeed, sir," answered Trescott. "This case has stood at a standstill much too long. Or," he continued, "it did until your arrival, Mr. Holmes."

On their trip to the Bath Bridge Club, Watson proved an unbeliever. "It is inconceivable to me, Holmes, that a thief like Sacker could burn a priceless masterpiece like one of the Panamanian Girls."

Holmes seemed indisposed to talk about the case. "If he did, Watson, my theory regarding these strange doings is certainly in ashes."

If Sherlock Holmes was disappointed by the bizarre turn of events, there was no indication that afternoon when he and Watson took their places at the table carefully placed in the exact center of the largest gaming room in the Bath Bridge Club. The Duke of Cumberland informed the kibitzers who crowded the room that strict silence was to be preserved during the play with no comments or revealing gestures. And so, the Challenge Match was resumed in its new locale.

SKURRY
♠ Q 8 5 3
♡ K Q 10 8 3
◊ J 6
♣ 8 5

HOLMES (Dealer)
♠ K 6 4
♡ A J 6 2
◊ A K 5
♣ Q 9 4

WATSON
♠ A 7 2
♡ 5
◊ 10 8 4 2
♣ A J 10 6 2

CASTLE
♠ J 10 9
♡ 9 7 4
◊ Q 9 7 3
♣ K 7 3

CHALLENGE MATCH BIDDING: (Holmes-Watson vulnerable)

Holmes	Skurry	Watson	Castle
1 NT	pass	3 NT	pass
pass	pass		

Holmes' opening bid was obvious. While Watson was worried about his singleton heart, he hoped his partner could bring in his good club suit and he went to game promptly.

With Harry's heart king on the table, Holmes played dummy's only card in the red major. Betty played the heart-four and Holmes played his heart-six. The Duke of

Cumberland exchanged a glance of mystification with a friend on his right at this point.

Skurry, noting that the heart-two was not in evidence, felt Betty might be signalling him and continued with the heart queen. This was all Holmes needed. Taking the queen with his ace, he promptly laid down the club queen. Betty took the trick but now her heart return could not hurt Holmes. He rapidly took four club tricks, two diamond tricks, two spade tricks and another trick in the heart suit for a ten-trick total.

There were dignified calls of "Bravo!" from the kibitzers. The Duke was the first to congratulate the detective.

"Mr. Holmes, what an ingenious play! Holding the heart ace-jack, I would have taken the first trick."

"Then I fear you would have gone down," replied Holmes with a smile. "If the club finesse is successful, ten tricks are readily available. However, as the cards lay, if I had taken the first trick and played the club queen, Betty would have taken it and returned the heart-nine. My exposed jack would have been trapped, the defense would have taken four tricks in the suit and the contract would have been defeated."

The Duke nodded, recognizing the logic in Holmes' words.

"This kind of bridge is, I fear, quite beyond us. Does this play have a name?"

"Not to my knowledge," replied Holmes. "My partner, Doctor Watson, is very adept at naming plays, but on this occasion perhaps I can suggest 'The Bath Coup.' "

All present were delighted at Holmes' suggestion, and the story was so well-circulated that, to this day, "The Bath Coup" has been the name for this type of Hold-up Play.

Strangely, the newly-named "Bath Coup" appeared

again during the afternoon session of play, but under different conditions.

HOLMES
♠ A Q J 6
♡ 5
♢ J 9 6 4
♣ K Q 10 3

CASTLE (Dealer)
♠ K 7
♡ A K 10 7 3
♢ A 8 2
♣ A J 2

SKURRY
♠ 9 4 2
♡ Q J 8 4
♢ K Q 3
♣ 8 7 5

WATSON
♠ 10 8 5 3
♡ 9 6 2
♢ 10 7 5
♣ 9 6 4

CHALLENGE MATCH BIDDING: (Skurry-Castle vulnerable)

Castle	Holmes	Skurry	Watson
1 ♡	double	2 ♡	pass
4 ♡	pass	pass	pass

Holmes' double was for take-out showing an opening bid, normally short of hearts. Betty, with her robust holding, was prepared to go to game if Harry made any raise at all.

When Holmes led the club king, Betty Castle took time out to plan her play. The lead and Holmes' takeout double made it apparent he held the two critical cards, the club queen and the spade ace. The loss of two clubs and two spades would, of course, set the four heart contract.

With "The Bath Coup" hand very fresh in her mind, Betty played low to the club king lead, hoping Holmes would continue the suit and allow her club ace-jack to win two tricks. It was another Bath Coup situation and Betty was alert to it. But so was Holmes. Watson played the club-four. Holmes could see the club-two in dummy and the club-three in his hand and knew his partner had played his lowest card. Holding the jack of the suit, Watson would have made a positive signal. Holmes shifted to the diamond-four on the second trick.

Betty's lips tightened when her trap was successfully avoided. But she did know who held the club queen and suddenly she saw the chance for a telling counterblow.

Betty won the diamond lead with dummy's queen and played three rounds of trumps. She then played out her good diamond tricks and said, with a smile: "Now, Mr. Holmes, since you wouldn't continue the club suit, I'm going to do it for you." With this, she led out the club ace and the club jack.

Holmes was stuck as he won the club jack with his queen. If he led another club or diamond, Betty would ruff in dummy and discard a losing spade from her hand. Holmes gave up gracefully, leading his spade ace and then the queen to Betty's king.

As the hand was being scored, Holmes complimented Betty on her excellent play. Baron Rothstone who had been kibitzing the lady said, with admiration: "It was like a fencing match. Thrust and parry."

"Actually," said Holmes, "Betty stripped my hand of safe exit cards and then threw me into the lead at a time when I was forced to do her work for her. A rather good name, don't you think? 'The Strip and Throw-in Play'?"

Betty colored slightly. "Why, Mr. Holmes, that sounds a little risqué. Could we not call it the 'Castle Coup'?"

But the "Strip and Throw-in" also called the "Strip and End Play" was on its way to join the growing vocabulary of bridge.

At the conclusion of the afternoon play, an excited Fenwick Trescott awaited Holmes and Watson at the door to the Bath Bridge Club. The triumphant look on his face told all. "We've found it, Mr. Holmes, just like you said—in the corner of the public park near the pond."

"I want to examine those ashes right away," said Holmes.

"They are at the station now," replied Trescott.

As Holmes' features registered exasperation, the Chief Constable quickly reassured him. "Either he was careless or that frame didn't burn the way he figured, Mr. Holmes. We've got one piece we can definitely identify. Mr. Ehrlenvale has already done so."

Holmes relaxed with satisfaction. "Excellent Trescott." Looking at Watson, with a grim smile, he continued: "Now we have the tools to force our way into the mind of Mr. Oswald Sacker."

Holmes' confidence was not shared by cracksman Sacker when he was faced by the master sleuth in his cell. His eyes widened in momentary alarm but then the ferret-like man leaned back in the bunk of his cell with a confident sneer.

"Look 'er who they brought down from Lon'on to see old Sacker—none other than the great 'Olmes," he said. Then he swung suddenly to his feet and shoved his face towards Chief Constable Trescott with a satisfied leer.

"You blew it for sure, Peeler. Now I got me a witness." His shifty eyes returned to Holmes. "Listen 'ere, Mr.

'Olmes, these country bumpkins 'as been 'olding me prisoner with no charge and no hevidence. My solicitor is going. . . ."

Sacker's voice dwindled away before the look on Holmes' face. There was something in the finality of those hawk-like features that gagged his bluster.

"You've had it, Sacker," stated Holmes. "Those ashes on your shoes—that was the first mistake. I analyzed them, naturally, and that led to our finding what was left of the painting you burned."

Suddenly, Sacker's face became pale, nay, pasty. Holmes continued to grind him under inexorably.

"A piece of the picture frame has already been identified." Turning to Watson, Holmes said, calmly: "Doctor, would you please bring the solution."

Following a rehearsed and pre-arranged procedure, Watson left the cell momentarily and then returned with a basin filled with an ill-smelling liquid. Calmly, he handed the basin to Trescott and passed some cotton swabbing to Holmes. The detective immersed the swabbing briefly in the basin and then crossed to the cracksman who was regarding him with eyes that mirrored terror.

"Put out your hands, Sacker."

" 'Ere now, wot's goin' on?"

"It won't hurt you," replied Holmes. His steely eyes seemed to hold the cracksman transfixed. Methodically Holmes passed the swabbing over the palms of both of Sacker's hands. "That should do it," he said with satisfaction and handed the swabbing back to Watson who looked very stern. "We can both analyze these later, doctor."

Sacker tried to say something but only a gurgle came out.

Holmes regarded him almost with pity.

"Did you know, Sacker, that fingerprints aren't the only sure means of identification. Now you take the saline solution on your hands."

Mystified, the cracksman regarded his now clean palms.

"If the saline solution on that hacksaw and jimmy and your other little toys match the sample I just took, we can prove you used them. We've got what's left of the painting. We've got the tools. And we've got you!"

Suddenly, the cracksman broke. Sinking back on the metal cell bunk he buried his face in his hands.

"All right, 'Olmes. Like you say, I've 'ad it." Suddenly, he looked up. "But 'ow in blazes you found them tools I don't figger. That pond is deep."

"Not as deep as you thought," said Trescott casually.

"Let's hear the story, Sacker," said Holmes.

All the starch had gone from the little man.

"I done the bit just like the others—the Grimes robbery—the Von Zeyffertitz house. . . ."

"How about Victor Selkirk's?"

"I don't know nuthin' about no Selkirk. You can't pin that one on me. I cracked the Ehrlenvale place and nabbed the picture of the woman and got away quick and burned it. It was the same routine—all three jobs. I should 've figgered it were too easy to last."

Holmes regarded the broken man keenly. "Burning art masterpieces is hardly in your line, Sacker. Who paid you?"

A fleeting look of satisfaction crossed the face of the cracksman.

"I can't tell you, Mr. Sherlock 'Olmes, wot I don't know. I got me orders by mail. 'Arf payment in advance, 'arf after the job was done. I signalled agreement with a code line in the Hagony Column of the London Sentinel. I wouldn't 'ave taken the first job but I figgered if I didn't 'ave no paintin' on me 'ands, there was no hevidence. And that's all I knows."

And it was. Holmes, Watson, and a downcast Trescott could learn no more from the burglar. As they made to leave his cell, Sacker had a question of his own.

"Wot was that you said, 'Olmes, about the saline somethin' on me 'ands?"

The great detective was always willing to discuss criminology with someone who possessed knowledge of the subject.

"The human hand carries a faint residue of salt due to perspiration," he stated. "It has long been a theory of mine that this could provide a means of identification."

"Theory?" yelled the cracksman. "You mean you can't do it?"

"Not yet," admitted Holmes with a twinkle in his steely eyes.

"But . . ." sputtered Sacker, "there's somethin' fishy 'ere. 'Ow'd you find them tools anyway?"

"You told us," replied Holmes. "We will find them. After all, we know where they are now."

Sacker groaned. "It's just as well I'm goin' for a long stretch. It's gettin' so an honest crook ain't got no chance!"

In Trescott's office, Holmes admitted that he was completely baffled by the turn of events. "Instead of theft for possession, my original concept of this case, we seem to be faced with a systematic destruction of all four paintings."

"The work of a madman?" hazarded Watson.

"Possibly," said the detective. "A relative of the former Lady Duncan—an enemy of the artist, Lansing—who knows?"

Trescott had his thief but he well knew, as did Holmes and Watson, that the case was far from closed.

The following morning at ten A.M., the Challenge Match got under way again. The seating accommodations in the gaming room were strained by kibitzers, eager to view this crack London bridge foursome and to see if Sherlock Holmes could come up with another new and startling bit of bridge legerdemain.

The great card-playing detective did not disappoint them.

SKURRY
♠ 6 2
♡ A K Q 9 7 4 3
◇ 10 7
♣ J 6

HOLMES (Dealer)
♠ A J 10 7 3
♡ 10 6 2
◇ A 6
♣ K 7 2

WATSON
♠ K Q 8 5
♡ J 8 5
◇ K 5 3
♣ A 4 3

CASTLE
♠ 9 4
♡ void
◇ Q J 9 8 4 2
♣ Q 10 9 8 5

CHALLENGE MATCH BIDDING: (neither side vulnerable)

Holmes	Skurry	Watson	Castle
1 ♠	4 ♡	4 ♠	pass
pass	pass		

Skurry's leap to four hearts was the weak jump overcall designed to show a long suit but poor outside high card strength.

Watson, with an opening bid of his own, bid game and

hoped that his partnership was not being pre-empted out of a slam.

Skurry leads three high hearts, then shifts to the diamond-10. Holmes was quite disappointed to find Watson with three heart cards and was obliged to lose the first three tricks to Skurry's high cards in this suit. Holmes' low club, with no place to put it, made the defeat of the game contract almost certain.

But Holmes wasn't ready to give up. He saw one distributional possibility that could give him his contract and like all experts he played as though he knew the favorable distribution actually existed.

Holmes was in hopes that Skurry held no more than two cards in each of the minor suits. In this case, Betty Castle would be obliged to guard diamonds and clubs.

For his fourth lead, Skurry played the diamond-10 which Holmes won with his ace. Then the detective played out five rounds of trumps discarding dummy's club-three.

On the lead of the final trump, Betty was obliged to bring her hand down to four cards. She held on to two diamonds and two clubs which turned Holmes' third club into a winning trick. Had Betty held on to three clubs and one diamond, dummy's low diamond would have become a winner.

As Holmes explained to the Duke: "It wasn't necessary to remember all the cards played. A count of one suit was enough."

In playing the hand, Holmes elected to carefully count all the clubs discarded. Toward the end when he played the club ace and then led low to the king, he knew his club-seven was a thirteener. If another club remained at large, Holmes was prepared to lead to dummy's diamond king and then play the low diamond.

This play is now called "The Automatic Squeeze"

since it works with many combinations where only one opponent is able to guard two suits.

HOLMES
♠ K J 7 2
♡ K J 10 8
♢ 6 4 3
♣ Q 4

SKURRY (Dealer)	CASTLE
♠ void	♠ 9 8 5 3
♡ 9 6 4 3	♡ A 5 2
♢ A K 9 8 7 5 2	♢ Q J 10
♣ 10 9	♣ A K 6

WATSON
♠ A Q 10 6 4
♡ Q 7
♢ void
♣ J 8 7 5 3 2

CHALLENGE MATCH BIDDING: (neither side vulnerable)

Skurry	Holmes	Castle	Watson
3 ♢	pass	5 ♢	pass
pass	pass		

Skurry's three diamond bid showed a seven card, or longer, suit, and the ability to win about six tricks in his own hand. Betty gambled that her hand would produce five tricks. Also, she wanted to shut out any interference bids.

From the bidding, Holmes reasoned that Skurry would find it necessary to gain a trick or two by ruffing in dummy. Hence his opening trump lead.

Skurry was greatly disappointed when Doctor Watson showed out of diamonds on the opening lead. However, his experienced mind spotted the danger suit. Realizing he could not afford to lose three heart tricks, he saw just two possibilities. The six missing hearts might break three-three. Or, if the heart distribution was not favorable, perhaps Doctor Watson would be forced to win the second or third heart lead. With this in mind Skurry played the heart ace and then a low heart card. Holmes overtook Doctor Watson's heart queen with his king and returned another trump.

On winning the second trump lead, with dummy's jack, Skurry led the third round of hearts. Unfortunately, Watson showed out and Holmes won the trick and erased Skurry's chances by returning the third round of the trump suit.

After going set, Skurry eyed Holmes with admiration. "Mr. Holmes, that was a brilliant opening lead. In fact, the opening of any suit except trumps allows me to make my contract with ease. However, I shouldn't complain." Skurry regarded his partner with some triumph. "Our opponents had a cold spade game and it cost us only 50 points."

Sherlock Holmes' eyes sparkled. "My dear Skurry, your problem was not to keep us from making a game. Rather it was to suppress your declarer role and play the pat of dummy."

"What do you mean?" sharply demanded Skurry.

"Let's reproduce Betty's hand," said Holmes.

CASTLE
♠ 9 8 5 3
♡ A 5 2
◇ Q J 10
♣ A K 6

"Now you hold seven diamonds, no spades and only two clubs. With the opening trump lead, Betty's hand has five usable entries. What would happen if you play your hand as the dummy and Betty's holding as the master hand? If you, as dummy, ruff Betty's four spades and the third club, what's left to lose?"

Skurry paused a few moments, then exclaimed: "By thunder, there're just two heart losers! Five diamonds can be made easily that way. Holmes, you have just invented a new reversal of dummy play."

The Duke of Cumberland, Baron Rothstone, and the kibitzers had been hanging on every word of the discussion and now waxed enthusiastic.

"What a smashing idea!" said the Duke. "'The Dummy Reversal.' And not so hard to figure, either. You just reverse your thinking."

Noting that Holmes was gazing at him with a fixed stare, the Duke continued: "I mean, one just imagines the declarer's hand as the dummy and the reverse. Don't you agree, Mr. Holmes?"

"I couldn't agree more, sir," stated Holmes.

The detective then requested a moment's pause in the match and left the room. When he returned, it seemed to

Watson that a load had been lifted from Holmes' shoulders.

SKURRY (Dealer)
♠ Q J 8
♡ K 9 6 5 2
◇ 6
♣ K Q J 5

HOLMES
♠ 9 5 2
♡ 4
◇ A 10 8 5 3
♣ 9 7 4 3

WATSON
♠ A K 7
♡ A 10 8 3
◇ 7 4 2
♣ A 6 2

CASTLE
♠ 10 6 4 3
♡ Q J 7
◇ K Q J 9
♣ 10 8

CHALLENGE MATCH BIDDING: (neither side vulnerable)

Holmes	Skurry	Watson	Castle
—	1 ♡	1 NT	double
2 ◇	pass	pass	double
pass	pass	pass	

Doctor Watson's overcall of one notrump promised the same high-card strength that an opening notrump guarantees. Actually, Watson's hand was one point light. He rationalized this with the fact that his heart holding, directly over the heart bidder, provided two likely stoppers.

Holmes realized his hand would probably produce but

one trick if played at notrump but several if played at a trump contract.

Betty Castle's doubles were based on her nine high card points plus Skurry's opening bid which should provide her side with more than one-half of the high card strength of the deck.

Skurry, like many expert players, belonged to the school that normally lead a trump whenever partner doubles a low level trump contract. Hence his lead of the diamond-six.

Holmes took the time to carefully count his likely winners and losers and then captured Betty's diamond jack with his ace. His plan was to make four trump tricks in spite of the missing trump honors.

The first step was a heart to dummy's ace and a heart return which Holmes ruffed in the closed hand. The spade ace and king provided two more entries to dummy for two more heart leads.

On the fourth heart lead, Betty was on the horns of a dilemma. She could ruff high which would promote Holmes' diamond-10 into a winner or she could discard which would give Holmes his fourth trump trick via another successful ruff. She elected to ruff with her diamond queen and then played the diamond king and nine-spot, removing all remaining trump cards. However, Holmes' diamond-10 and club ace completed the eight tricks necessary to fulfill his doubled contract.

Watson, so sensitive to the moods of his old friend, could hardly wait until the Challenge Match contestants broke for lunch. When he buttonholed the sleuth in private, Holmes greeted him with a wry laugh.

"You can write me down an ass this time, Watson," he said. "Regarding the mystery of the Panamanian Girl paintings, I have been a dolt indeed," continued Holmes. "It took a remark of the Duke to awaken me from my stupor. You will recall, Watson, that he said: 'You just reverse your thinking.' "

With a wince, Holmes continued: "In this case of art thievery, I assumed it was motivated by a desire for possession and I was right there. But I was looking at all the clues the wrong way. The fallacy in my reasoning was that the paintings had hung in Duncan Castle for thirty years and had never been stolen. Who was the one man most obsessed with the idea of owning the Panamanian Girls? Why, Lord Duncan himself. Finally, driven to the wall by financial problems, he sold one to Victor Selkirk. But he sold a copy, Watson, and probably lay awake nights wondering when his deceit would be exposed. Then, by happenstance, the Selkirk mansion burned to the ground and the evidence that Duncan feared burned with it. This is what gave him the idea of the three following thefts. He stole the copies to prevent exposure.

"Why, it all fits together," said Watson excitedly. "He never sold to a museum or gallery but always to individuals, most often new to great wealth and not art fanciers."

"The clues were staring at me, Watson," said Holmes sadly. "I just had to change my point of view."

At the end of the day's play, a message arrived from Chief Constable Fenwick Trescott which signalled the end of the Panamanian Girls adventure. Lord Duncan, at Holmes' suggestion, had been decoyed away from his castle and a search squad of constables had unearthed the genuine paintings in a secret room which had been used by the Duncans during the religious wars.

Holmes was reluctant to ever discuss this case, which he personally listed among his failures. No doubt this explains why his involvement in the complex affair is only known through Watson's "Diary of the Challenge Match."

In the "Diary," there is a rather wistful memo that Watson never did get to see the cause of the whole matter—the four unbelievably lovely Panamanian Girls. Some margin notes in the "Diary" do indicate that the doctor left Bath with regrets. Much of this is surmise since the notes are very sketchy but there are grounds for the assumption that Doctor Watson became quite interested in a kibitzer of the match at the Bath Bridge Club. Supposedly, said kibitzer was a striking blond lady, Miss Dorothy Hoyden of Croyden. However, no reference to her is made in the "Diary of the Challenge Match" after the participants returned to the familiar surroundings of the Grosvenor Bridge Club. It would seem that nothing ever came of this association.

Holmes and Watson's lead in the match was somewhat narrower than when they left London, but the great detective seemed to be in excellent health again. There was another and far-reaching benefit from the trip to Bath. Taking the match outside metropolitan London, even briefly, did much to popularize the game throughout England. Chief Constable Fenwick Trescott became an avid bridge player and in later years formed a strong partnership with one H. Ewing-Belsey of Scotland.

The Exploits of Androcles MacThick: Or a Club to A-void

By Ernst T. Theimer

THE Rev. E. S. Bulcon was an amazing personality with one outstanding characteristic at the bridge table which made him completely inexplicable unless one looked at him backward. What happened the night of his encounter with Androcles MacThick, the great Australian expert, can be explained only by the latter's dominant personality which, as usual, prevailed even in these most unusual circumstances.

Born of thespian parents in the classical tradition, he was christened Euripides Sophocles Bulcon, and naturally became "E. S." during his school-days and at the university. Upon graduation from divinity school he became the Rev. E. S. Bulcon, which may or may not account for his peculiar affliction which made this story possible. His acceptance of the post of pastor of a church in the town of Keintreff was, no doubt, the clincher.

It was at the airport in Keintreff that Andy MacThick found himself at loose ends. He had been visiting his nephew Archy on a stop-over on his way to the Nationals and had booked an early evening flight. However, a fog had settled over the area and all flights were delayed. Although it was expected that service would be resumed, it might be a matter of some hours and all passengers were asked to stand by.

Andy wandered around the terminal, which was a large building containing, in addition to the usual services, a community center which was a gathering place for much of the population of the town. After exhausting the attractions of the newsstands, and the bowling and billiard areas, he pushed open the door at the end of a corridor and found that his unerring instinct had brought him into the headquarters of the local bridge club. Introductions revealed that the man who was just laying out the boards for the evening tournament was Frank Chase, the tournament director, who was much impressed to have such a famous personality as Andy MacThick come to his modest establishment. Chase had originally planned to play with young Joe Parks, a comparative beginner, but Joe assured them that he would prefer to watch and learn, so it was arranged that Andy would play with the director after checking in with the airline to report his whereabouts. There was a brief discussion of the system they would play, and as the players began straggling in Andy settled himself for an enjoyable evening.

"The only trouble," said Chase slowly, "is that the Pastor is playing tonight."

"I beg your pardon?"

"The Rev. E. S. Bulcon. We let him play once a month and tonight is his night."

"What has that to do with me?"

"Do you mean to say you never heard of Rev. Bulcon?"

"No, I haven't." Andy was growing a bit impatient. "I

must say I haven't the slightest idea what you are talking about."

"I suppose that you, like all the others, won't believe it at first," said Chase, "but you'll soon see it with your own eyes, so I may as well give you the thing straight. You see, E. S. is one of the best bridge players in these parts, but he messes up every game he plays in, because he never holds any clubs."

He paused to let his words sink in. Andy looked intently at the man. Yes, he seemed normal enough, even though somewhat harassed. And young Parks, scarcely out of his teens, did not seem the least perturbed by the manager's pronouncement.

"We noticed it right from the start," continued Chase. "Rubber bridge or duplicate—it made no difference. He just never picked up any clubs. I can't explain it, of course. It just doesn't make sense, but it's a fact, and it spoils every contest, because the others all know that every deal will have one hand void in clubs—the hand that E. S. has held or will hold later. E. S. can't play in sectional events or in the Nationals for it would upset the whole tournament, but we all like him here at home, and we let him play once a month in our duplicate because he loves the game so much."

"If this is a joke," thought Andy, "but no, after all, I'm going to play tonight, and any hoax would be just too obvious." However, he was still bewildered. "Didn't you ever rig a hand, when you were phantom, for instance?," he asked. "It seems such an obvious way to cross up this jinx or whatever you wish to call it."

"We tried that once. The Reverend was to get a fixed hand on the tenth round. Everyone who played in that duplicate and got the normal hand was warned, so as not to give away the show. However, about ten o'clock that night the clubhouse burned down, and we couldn't finish the tournament. We never tried *that* again!"

By this time many players had arrived, including Bulcon himself, who walked in with a sort of apologetic air, as if he were sorry he was causing everyone so much trouble and hoped nobody would mind too much if he played that evening; after all, could he help it if he just never managed to pick up a club, no matter how hard he tried?

"E. S." seemed a nice enough young fellow with his shaggy brown hair and long awkward legs. He took his place at the anchor table and the director began to distribute the boards.

"E. S. always sits stationary in the North position," he explained. "That way everyone knows automatically that all the North hands will be void in clubs, and it saves a lot of unnecessary confusion. It's only fair that each player has the same advantage as the people at E. S.' table."

The matter-of-fact way in which Chase talked about this amazing phenomenon made Andy giddy. It still didn't seem possible—but the game was about to begin. The boards were shuffled, and he sat down opposite the director and began to play. It was immediately apparent that his partner was an excellent player, and there was every indication that the game would be most enjoyable. Also, after a few rounds Andy discovered that all the players seemed very capable—far above the average expectancy for a small town duplicate. But most amazing by far was the fact that the story of Rev. Bulcon was the plain, unvarnished truth, for every North hand was entirely void of the club suit.

The novel problems that these situations presented to Andy challenged even that astute individual's brilliant mind, and gave him a real workout. In fact, afterwards he admitted that some of the hands were the most amazing he had ever encountered.

The very first round produced a gem.

Both vulnerable
South deals

North
♠ Q 9 7 6
♡ 9 8 7 6 3
♢ Q 10 9 7
♣ - - - -

West
♠ J 4
♡ A 10
♢ A 5 4 3 2
♣ A 8 7 5

East
♠ A K 10 8 5 2
♡ K 5 4 2
♢ K 8 6
♣ - - - -

South
♠ 3
♡ Q J
♢ J
♣ K Q J 10 9 6 4 3 2

South	West	North	East
3 ♣	3 ♢	Pass	4 ♣
Dbl	Rdbl	Pass	4 ♠
5 ♣	Dbl	Pass	5 ♡
Pass	6 NT	(end)	

As soon as the dealer opened the bidding, Andy started in amazement, for South had found, of all things, a three club bid, even though vulnerable, and with a partner he knew to have no clubs. Having been assured that the bid had no special significance, Andy, with three tricks, bid three diamonds, not caring particularly whether his partner construed this as Cholmondeley (Australian version of Fishbein). North passed, and Chase now bid four clubs, which South doubled.

"Apparently a cue-bid," thought MacThick, "but a bit of a strain to put on a new partnership, particularly in this hellish situation. I'll just pass the ball right back to him." And he redoubled, hoping that would show the Ace.

Chase seemed disappointed by this obvious duplication of values, and settled for a game bid, so when South persisted with his clubs, Andy doubled, confident he would get an adequate penalty. His partner was not so sure, however, and can hardly be blamed for now going five hearts. After all, West ought to have support for at least one of the majors. And now Andy, deprived of his 800 point set, decided he would try for equivalent value, and contracted for the no-trump slam.

North led the nine of hearts, and when dummy went down, Andy saw that he had no lay-down for twelve tricks. After checking to make sure that his partner had not suddenly become the Rev. Bulcon, he set about planning the hand. Spades had to be brought in whole in any case, otherwise there was no hope, and even then there were only eleven top tricks. Since South had nine clubs, the best bet was to play North for everything in spades, so the heart was won with the Ace, South putting up the Jack. The spade Jack was led and North made things more difficult by covering, for now Andy had to use up his last entry, the Ace of diamonds, to return to his hand. When South followed to this trick, however, Andy could practically spread the hand. For in addition to his nine clubs, South almost surely had the Queen of hearts left to complete his holding.

So the four of spades was led, and the eight spot finessed. Andy now had eleven tricks, one of which was in the entryless West hand, but he was not worried, because South was going to be very obliging and give him an entry and squeeze his partner all at the same time.

The spades were run, with South discarding clubs. He had to hold the heart Queen, else the ten spot would have been the eleventh trick as well as an entry to the club Ace for the twelfth. After the run of spades, this was the situation:

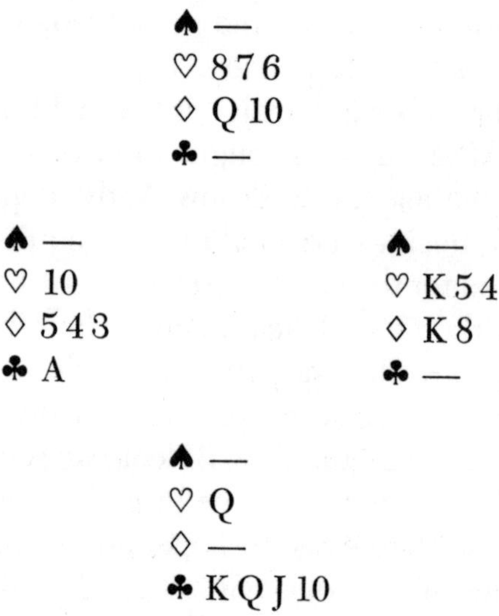

Now Andy underled his heart King, playing the four to South's Queen, and when the latter perforce returned a club to put Andy on lead, he at the same time squeezed North who had to unguard one of his red suits, giving declarer the rest of the tricks.

By this time all the other tables were ready for the

next round, but if Andy hoped for a respite he was sadly mistaken. The very first board of the new round produced the big brother of the imp he had just subdued.

E-W VULNERABLE
SOUTH DEALS

NORTH
♠ J 10 8 7 5
♡ K 7 6 5
◇ Q 5 4 3
♣ —

WEST
♠ 6 2
♡ 10 9 4 3
◇ A
♣ A K 5 4 3 2

EAST
♠ A K 9
♡ A Q
◇ K J 10 2
♣ Q 8 7 6

SOUTH
♠ Q 4 3
♡ J 8 2
◇ 9 8 7 6
♣ J 10 9

SOUTH	WEST	NORTH	EAST
Pass	1 ♣	Pass	2 ◇
Pass	3 ♣	Pass	6 NT
(end)			

Again Andy heard his partner's opening bid with some astonishment, as he considered his own substantial holding. He forced with two diamonds and jumped directly to slam when Chase confirmed the club suit, for any potentially outstanding honor would likely be finessable.

South led the nine of diamonds which was taken by

the singleton Ace. Andy quickly counted six clubs, two diamonds, a heart, and two spades for eleven. A beginner might try the heart finesse for the twelfth trick, but a better player would not take the gamble. He would rather enter the East hand and lead the King and Jack of diamonds, forcing out the Queen. This would give him his twelfth trick with the diamond ten, but nevertheless to his pain and sorrow he would not make the hand.

Andy saw the joker just in time. North being void in clubs, *the suit was bound to block!* There was apparently no way to avoid a club loser without abandoning the long cards in the suit, but it was abundantly obvious that without the entire club suit there would be no slam. So Andy took the only chance, which required North to have the heart King and South the Jack—a one-in-four shot. At trick two, before even a single fatal round of clubs, he led a small heart and finessed the Queen. The circle had been completed, and the expert had taken the beginner's play, but for good and sufficient reason. Now the heart Ace was cashed, and dummy was entered with the Ace of clubs. Finally, on the ten of hearts Andy discarded the annoying six of clubs, and the contract was safe. Either opponent could win the trick, but that was all, and justice emerged triumphant. For the slam was surely not unreasonable and without the complication in clubs it would have been a laydown. Therefore, it was only fair that the alternate chance should have worked. But, without advance knowledge that North held no clubs, declarer would have gone down, for playing even one round of that suit would have destroyed communications, and the hearts could no longer have been used in the required manner.

The director was most lavish in his praise of Andy's fine play, and young Parks watched with obvious awe.

Even the opponents were suitably impressed. The master player felt a glow of satisfaction at the genuine appreciation shown by this fine group of people.

The next few boards were not too spectacular, and gave Andy a slight breather which was greatly appreciated considering the monstrosity that appeared soon afterwards.

N-S VULNERABLE
EAST DEALS

NORTH
♠ J 9 8 6 5 4 2
♡ 8
◇ J 6 5 4 3
♣ —

WEST
♠ A K
♡ A K Q J 6 4
◇ 9
♣ A 8 5 2

EAST
♠ Q 3
♡ 10 9
◇ A K Q 8 7 2
♣ 9 6 3

SOUTH
♠ 10 7
♡ 7 5 3 2
◇ 10
♣ K Q J 10 7 4

EAST	SOUTH	WEST	NORTH
Pass	Pass	2 ♡	Pass
3 ◇	Pass	3 ♡	Pass
4 ◇	Pass	4 ♡	Pass
5 ♡	Pass	6 ♡	(end)

North led a small diamond and Andy's laydown slam was converted into a real problem. He won the Ace of diamonds, but his side entry was now gone, and there were some losing clubs to consider. His first impulse was to play the nine and ten of trumps, then to lead diamonds, hoping either for an even diamond split, or the inability of the hand with short diamonds to ruff.

However, consideration showed that this was far from the best procedure. For it would lose whenever one opponent had three or four trumps and less than three diamonds. On the other hand, playing diamonds immediately would win in every case where drawing two rounds of trumps would work, and in many other cases besides. (If the diamonds were 4-2, all was well, as long as Andy threw the spade King on the second diamond, and if North had but one diamond, the hand was hopeless, for he would now have at least three hearts, as he was void in clubs.)

Andy led the King of diamonds to trick two, and South ruffed. Andy overruffed with the Jack, cashed the Ace of spades, and led a small heart to the nine, continuing with the Queen of diamonds. South was now helpless, but actually he threw a club, and Andy discarded his King of spades. (If he had not cashed the Ace previously, he would have been set by South's refusal to ruff.) Next the eight of diamonds was led, and South again discarded a club. Andy, who had been forced to trump a high diamond, now permitted the losing diamond to ride, discarding a club. North was now end-played—whatever card he led put the lead in dummy, and as soon as South ruffed, he was overruffed and a low heart to dummy's ten spot drew East's last trump. The remaining high cards in dummy were just sufficient to provide declarer with the necessary discards.

"There seems to be an unusual number of slams tonight," said the Australian Master. "It would be a relief to get a simple game hand, where one could afford to lose a few tricks!"

Part of this wish was immediately granted. Andy got his game contract on the next hand, which turned out to be tougher than any previous deal, and also more remarkable.

BOTH VULNERABLE
WEST DEALS

	NORTH	
	♠ K Q J 10 9 6 3 2	
	♡ 3 2	
	◇ K 7 2	
	♣ ---	
WEST		EAST
♠ 5		♠ A 8
♡ A K		♡ J 10 5
◇ Q J 10		◇ A 9 8 5 4 3
♣ Q 9 7 6 5 3 2		♣ K 4
	SOUTH	
	♠ 7 4	
	♡ Q 9 8 7 6 4	
	◇ 6	
	♣ A J 10 8	

WEST	NORTH	EAST	SOUTH
1 ♣	1 ♠	2 ◇	2 ♡
Pass	2 ♠	3 ♠	Pass
3 NT	(end)		

When his partner cue-bid spades, Andy was faced with a problem. To try for game in clubs was obviously absurd, with all the adverse cards in that suit bunched in South's hand. Also, game in diamonds seemed remote, especially since South would be in a position to give his partner immediate ruffs in clubs. There was nothing left but to hope that the spade cue-bid indicated adequate stoppers in that suit and to bid game in no-trump on the basis of the two heart stoppers and the diamond fit.

North led the spade King and Andy sucked in his breath when he saw the dummy. With the spade Ace removed, there would be no entry to dummy. The diamonds were blocked automatically, so that even if North had the King, the suit could not be run. The only hope was for North to have at least eight spades, which was not too unlikely, considering his two vulnerable bids and his lack of tricks in the other suits.

Andy ducked the spade lead, a play which would have been necessary even if South had held only one. Now North, who knew that Andy knew that he was entryless, shifted to the three of hearts. It seemed as if this play gave declarer a respite, but that was an illusion, for a spade continuation would have simplified the play required to make the contract.

Dummy and South ducked, and Andy was in with the King of hearts to lead the ten of diamonds. If North had ducked, the play would again have been easier, but they were defending well that night, and North went right up with the King. It was now mighty tempting to duck, and thus to clear the diamonds. However, a heart return would have knocked out the Ace, and the contract would have been down one automatically. Andy could take two hearts, a spade, and five diamonds, but South would then win the first club lead and take the rest in hearts.

Androcles MacThick was not often at a loss at the bridge table. He had extricated himself from apparently hopeless situations on innumerable occasions, but just now he was in a quandary, for at first he could not see how to prevent his Ace of hearts from being driven out.

Suddenly he saw the light, and a queer smile came to his lips, for the irony of the solution appealed to his sense of humor. The way to prevent the heart Ace from being driven out was to DISCARD it. So the diamond King was taken with the Ace and the Ace of spades—that lovely bulwark against the formidable adverse suit—was cashed, and on it Andy threw his other bulwark, the Ace of hearts.

It was still possible to go astray. By playing the Jack of hearts, one of the blocking diamonds could have been discarded, and if South won with the Queen, he would have to put dummy on lead while permitting Andy to pitch the other diamond. However, if South refused to take the heart Jack, declarer would be "dead," so instead Andy merely cashed the Queen and Jack of diamonds, and then led a club to the King.

South had to win with the Ace and could now cash the heart Queen. When he then led the club Jack, he was permitted to hold his fourth and last trick, for he now had the choice of giving the remaining tricks to dummy in diamonds or to the closed hand in clubs.

Andy was beginning to feel as in a dream. He was discovering plays in bridge he had never before encountered. It was surely something new in his experience to discard a stopper in no-trump while cashing another stopper as the only way to make a contract. What would come next?

He found out several rounds later.

E-W VULNERABLE
SOUTH DEALS

NORTH
♠ 10 8 7 6 3 2
♡ K J 9 8 6
◇ Q J
♣ —

WEST
♠ —
♡ A Q 5 4 2
◇ A 7 3
♣ A 10 5 4 3

EAST
♠ K Q J 9 4
♡ 7 3
◇ K 5
♣ K Q 9 8

SOUTH
♠ A 5
♡ 10
◇ 10 9 8 6 4 2
♣ J 7 6 2

SOUTH	WEST	NORTH	EAST
3 ◇	3 ♡	Dbl	3 ♠
Pass	4 ♣	Pass	6 ♣
(end)			

South's three diamond bid was a typical non-vulnerable bid on "garbage." Against vulnerable opponents it had value as a nuisance bid, and ought to be safe enough. Actually, three diamonds can be set 700, but only with a trump lead or the Ace of hearts and a trump shift, either of which should net 900 points. However, Andy elected to try for the vulnerable game, and overcalled with three hearts. North doubled to indicate that he was prepared for spades as well as hearts—his partner was to keep still about his diamonds. Of course, everyone knew the club situation.

East did not care for hearts, but was, of course, perfectly content to get quite high at other contracts. The only question in his mind was about a slam. Andy, somewhat afraid that they were now out on a limb, was nevertheless forced to bid four in the "forbidden" club suit, and was greatly surprised to find himself in slam directly thereafter.

The opening lead was the Queen of diamonds. When the dummy went down, Andy saw that he had quite a problem. Normally, the best chance would be to ruff out the spade Ace, and hope for a favorable trump split; then by conceding a heart the remaining small cards in the closed hand could be taken care of with two pitches on spades and two ruffs. (The heart King was obviously off side and well protected.)

But in a Bulcon hand this was, of course, out of the question. South had all four clubs and at least six diamonds for his pre-empt. He thus had at most three cards in the majors.

If the spade Ace were blank in South's hand, the diamond could be won in dummy, and a small spade ruffed to catch the Ace. But now there would be no squeeze since either South would have to be let in with a diamond (as North would then have seven spades and at least five hearts, so only one diamond) to return a heart and break communications, or else a diamond could be ruffed in dummy, but in that case, however, trumps could not be drawn and declarer still wind up in dummy for the squeeze.

The only hope was for North to have the diamond Jack, in which case there would still be hope even if the spade Ace was protected.

The King of diamonds won the opening lead and the spade King was played. South covered and Andy ruffed. Now if he made the perfectly normal play of the Ace of diamonds followed by a diamond ruff in the short trump hand, the contract was doomed. In this amazing hand, the sure eleventh trick thus available had to be relinquished entirely. Furthermore, the Ace of diamonds could not be cashed, and even one round of clubs would wreck the slam.

Andy found the only chance. He led the seven of diamonds at the third trick! North, in with the Jack, was endplayed. If he led a heart, declarer would win, cash the diamond Ace, discarding the *spade four*, and cash all the clubs ending in dummy. On the last club, North would be squeezed in hearts and spades.

Actually, North led a spade, and Andy played the nine-spot from dummy. The only danger was that South had held the doubleton Ace-ten, but when the nine held, the hand was in.

A club was finessed, and a heart discarded on the diamond Ace. No attempt at a cross-ruff could succeed on the bidding, but now the same squeeze became operative. The ceded trick had been regained by the endplay, and when the clubs were all cashed North was squeezed in hearts and spades.

The attempt to ruff the third diamond fails because dummy becomes shortened in trumps. The only communication is in trumps and dummy must be as long as the West hand, for if there were a club residue in West at the time of the lead being in dummy, the North hand would not be down to the point where a "busy" card could be squeezed out. The play was thus the sacrifice of a sure trick which had to be regained by an endplay, either in hearts or spades, so that by maintaining trump equality in dummy, communication for a squeeze at the eleventh trick could be maintained.

"Partner," said Frank Chase, feelingly, "you're playing like an angel! One would think that you were a confirmed Bulconite."

Andy was pleased by the compliment but a little worried. "This is certainly a workout," he admitted, "and no end of fun. But I doubt the value as practice for the Nationals."

But the next deal was already at hand.

BOTH VULNERABLE
SOUTH DEALS

NORTH
♠ J 9 6
♡ 7 6 5 3 2
◇ J 10 8 7 6
♣ —

WEST
♠ 10 8 7 5 4 3 2
♡ A
◇ —
♣ K Q 8 5 4

EAST
♠ A K Q
♡ 9 8 4
◇ 9 5 4 3 2
♣ A 2

SOUTH
♠ —
♡ K Q J 10
◇ A K Q
♣ J 10 9 7 6 3

SOUTH	WEST	NORTH	EAST
1 ♡	2 ♠	4 ♡	4 ♠
6 ♡	6 ♠	(end)	

South opposite Bulcon did not even bother to mention his clubs, and after some spirited competitive bidding Andy wound up in the spade slam with North leading the seven of hearts. Chase spread the dummy and Andy considered his possibilities.

Just then the telephone rang in the private booth. It was the desk collecting all the stray passengers as the fog had lifted and the plane was leaving as soon as possible.

As Andy stood in the booth he glanced at the boards lying on the relay table near by. He noted idly that these were the hands which the Rev. Bulcon would play the next round. Suddenly gripped by an impulse, Andy reached out and smuggled one of the boards into the booth. Then making certain that no one had noticed, he quickly took out the cards, and sorted them into suits. After all, what matter one fouled board in a local duplicate, compared with a man's peace of mind? Andy's first impulse was to put all thirteen clubs into the North pocket. He was thinking vaguely of shock therapy, or perhaps of the healing value of overdoses of poisons, and "E. S." was going to be cured if it killed him. But finally he gave North the ten top clubs and put one in each of the other pockets, just in case the board got turned. North also got the Ace-King of spades and the Ace of hearts, but the Ace of diamonds went to West, just to make sure that Bulcon would have to play the hand at seven CLUBS.

Andy replaced the board without being seen and returned to the table.

"I have to leave," he apologized, "but I shall claim twelve tricks at my six spade contract, assuming only, from the lead and the bidding, that North has led the seven of hearts from top of nothing. In that case the hand is a laydown. Perhaps you would like to work it out for yourselves," he smiled, and scribbled a few words on a piece of paper. Shaking hands, he made his adieux. The director was sorry he had to leave, but Parks would take his place for the last few boards, and it would be all right.

Being true Bridge enthusiasts, the three at the table decided to work out the problem for themselves without looking at Andy's solution. With proper regard for that individual's ability they scored the slam as fulfilled and brought out the board for study after the tournament. In the early morning hours they solved the puzzle themselves along the lines of Andy's brief message and in so doing discovered yet another aspect of the wonderful world of squeezes.*

And so, Androcles MacThick walked out of the Keintreff Bridge Club, and out of the life of the Rev. E. S. Bulcon, his thoughts already turning to the National Championships and the excitements of master competition.

It must be admitted that for a while he had some anxious moments, and for several days he watched apprehensively for news of some disaster in the town of Keintreff. But the local papers of that section of the country made mention of no fire, earthquake, or other calamity, and Andy finally heaved a sigh of satisfaction at the successful emancipation of the bridge soul of E. S. Bulcon.

That is, until quite a few months later back home "down under," when his mail contained a badly crumpled letter which had apparently followed him halfway

* Andy's solution. Obviously if the spades are divided there is no problem. If South has all three, he must be void in diamonds and after trumps are drawn, a diamond is passed to North with a club discarded from West, setting up a squeeze on South. However, if North has all the spades, dummy is entered three times with trumps. The first two times diamonds are ruffed but on the third trip to dummy, South, regardless of his holding, must discard his last diamond and, again, the throw-in of North with a third diamond squeezes South in hearts and clubs for the twelfth trick.

around the world. It was from his erstwhile partner, Frank Chase.

"Dear MacThick," it read, "you are doubtless wondering how we finished that night in Keintreff. Well, I am sorry to admit we did not quite win, for young Parks bobbled a couple and knocked us out of top place. I am sure you will get over that disappointment, however.

"My main reason for writing you is, I suspect, no surprise. On the last round, Bulcon picked up a hand, turned pale, and flopped on the floor. When we brought him around, he bid and made seven clubs, for his holding was the ten top clubs, the Ace-King of spades, and the Ace of hearts. But I am sure you know that, for the hand was obviously rigged, and I draw my own conclusions from the proximity of the relay table to the telephone booth where you were standing.

"Anyway, your little plan worked, after a fashion, for ever since then the Reverend has held clubs quite normally, just like the rest of us, and so we would be most willing to welcome him into the fold of normal players. The only trouble is that, since that hand, he has always been void in diamonds!"

DATE DUE			